...

Twice Is Not Enough

...

Also by Che Chidi Chukwumerije

Prose:
The Lake of Love
There Is Always Something More

Poetry:
The Beautiful Ones Have Been Born
Writing Is The Happiness Of Sorrow
Palm Lines
River
Cumbrian Lines: poems born of the lake district
Light of Awakening

Non-english:
Mmiri a zoro nwayo nwayo (Poems written in igbo)
Der Schlaf, aus dem ich wachend träume (Poems written in german)
Innengart (Poems written in german)
Das dauerhafte Gedicht (Poems written in german)

For children:
Somayinozo's Stories

Che Chidi Chukwumerije
Twice Is Not Enough
Second Edition 2015.
First edition 2013 under the pseudonym Aka Teraka
Boxwood Publishing House e.K.
Copyright © Che Chidi Chukwumerije 2013
All rights reserved
ISBN 978-3-943000-82-5

CHE CHIDI CHUKWUMERIJE

...

Twice Is Not Enough

A Novella

...

Boxwood Publishing House, Frankfurt

Some love stories are like underground streams, constantly looking for an outlet to emerge into the sun.

The story of a struggling poet in love.

The harmattan winds, on their southwards journey from the Sahara to the Atlantic, paused one last time in Lagos, sometime between Christmas and New Year of 1998, to breathe its haze upon a never resting city and bind the hearts of four people in its nebulous spell. A chance encounter in a bus leads to the re-awakening of an old love, the forging of new bonds, the strengthening of hopes and the severing of ties.

The Chapters

Chapter 1	8
Chapter 2	30
Chapter 3	32
Chapter 4	44
Chapter 5	61
Chapter 6	77
Chapter 7	88
Chapter 8	90
Chapter 9	123

Whisperings

...

Whisperings of a new return of harmattan...
Is it hazy? Was it foggy? Dark, bright?
Feels, like Dawn, Sounds, like Dawn
Looks, like new Dawn –

An early breath of Harmattan serenaded
My heart –
Birds accompany, airy prose
Crickets nonstop chirping
Yet night is gone ~
Deeply I love the boundary between
Rains and thirsty Harmattan...

Nature has said yes,
Why say no?

...

The Chapters

...

Chapter 1

...

The poem had been going round and round in her head all morning. It had been with her when she arose and saw the haze through the window. It had been with her when she thought of her destination. But she had lost it now, in the middle, on the path between her beautiful beginning and the end of her journey. Now she was walking past the toughest, roughest, most chaotic, dirtiest market in her world and it had torn her out of her reverie. She would have much preferred not to come this way, but she had to, to get to the bus she needed.

The beautiful woman continued calmly down her path, ignoring the lusty cat-calls being pelted without restrain at her by the Oshodi traders. Rough young men with coarse voices and bad intentions. Given half a chance, they would make her regret not only her manner of dressing today, but that she even came this way at all, to this dirty, colourless, overpopulated market, to do her shopping.

Yet she walked with her head high, as though she were not burning with shame as she heard the phrases they were directing at her.

"Na me and you o! If I finish you, you no go want leave me lai-lai!"

"Baby you carry o! Me sef I carry. Come see am!"

Loud peals of dirty male laughter rolled after her. Her? Other people were following the scene with amusement. She walked as fast as she could without seeming to be in any hurry. There were other women, she knew, who would have returned insult for insult, thrown dirt for dirt, traded bad tongue for bad tongue, claimed an eye for an eye, verily, and a tooth for a tooth…. But *she* couldn't. She was above that, above them. So she silently breathed her humiliation, in and out, in and out, in and out.

Soon she was out of range of the insults. She was in the thick of the crowd now, marching with the faceless rhythm of those who work a lot and earn a little. The masses. Nobody paid any attention to her now. Everybody was walking fast, as though propelled by a common will. Now she relaxed, and as she let out that one big outflow of breath, for some reason a few tears accompanied it and blurred her vision. Surreptitiously her left hand came up to her eyes and, in one quick little motion, her thumb and forefinger, stroking inwards from the outer corners of both eyes, met at the top of the bridge of her nose, and her vision was restored. Yet she was angry.

She boarded the Molue and settled back uncomfortably between two market women on a seat that would surely have seated only two people conveniently, if convenience could ever be spoken of at all in connection with a Molue bus. But a fresh breeze sighed softly through the window as the bus gathered speed and left the hell-hole of a market behind.

After the cool breeze had relaxed her somewhat, her anger receded and her mind slipped out of the bus and travelled to her brother, the university drop-out. Having been rid of one set of anxieties, she was now besieged by an other and quite different one.

Tony.

Why couldn't he be like other people? Afterall he wasn't the only poet ever born, nor would he be the last, would he?

Thinking about Tony brought pain always to Ada's heart. If it wasn't the pain of disappointment, sorrow or worry, it was the pain of incomprehension and yearning.

She slipped her hand into her shopping bag by her feet and brought out the sheets of paper he had given her, a look of hope in his eyes, early that morning before she left for the market.

The Molue bus ambled and roared on. And what a roar. By now they had gone past the Air Force Barracks and were fast closing in on Ikeja Bus-stop, the outer. Because it was the middle of the day, there were not too many people at the intermediary bus-stops who were going their way.

Like a fruit ripening out of the skies, an ADC plane bore down, above and to the left of them, but fast and loud sinking, into the domestic airport behind the National Petrol Station on the other side of the road. One of the bus-conductors was already leaning out of one of the perpetually open doors of this Lagos road-monster, preparing to shout out his route and stops to the pedestrians waiting at the bus-stop.

Another conductor was guardedly, swiftly, unsmilingly moving from one seat to the other, collecting his fare.

He was soon by her seat. His rough hand quivered, open palm face-up, before the faces of the three women sitted there.

"Yes? *Owo da!*" His voice permitted of no negotiations. His eyes were fixed, heavy-laden, on Ada's exposed dark brown thighs. As she paid him, his eyes lifted a trifle and hers caught them. They stared at one another coolly for one moment, then he turned, his money in hand, to go.

"Ah-ah! *Changi mi da?*" the heavy-set woman on Ada's left called loudly at him.

"*Ma fun ẹ change, jọọ, durooo,*" he replied without turning back.

"Give me my change now! Ole! Thief!" she ejaculated poisonously at him.

Ada shifted a little to the side and stole a glance at

her from under the corner of her eye. The woman had a fleshy face that pinched in her eyes and weighed down the corners of her lips.

The conductor turned around and thrust a twenty naira note into her outstretched claws. As he turned to give her the money and then turned back again to continue with his fare-collection, his yellow-brown eyes slid back and forth again up and down and across Ada's full, exposed thighs, and there was a look in those eyes.

Instinctively, Ada locked her knees tightly together and haunched forward over her upper thighs. The woman to her left saw everything and, with an amused smile, turned her face away and pointed her eyes out of the open window. Now that she had collected her change, she could afford to be thus entertained even by the offshoots of the things the eyes of the same conductor now did, and in the back of the woman's throat Ada again heard the little dirty laugh. Why was Lagos so dirty?

Ada lifted her bag off the floor and lay it horizontally across her thighs, uncaged by her micro mini skirt. She extracted Tony's poems now from the bag, which action had been earlier interrupted by the conductor, the look in whose eyes she was trying to push out of her mind.

They were six long sheets, on each one poem. If only he had a job or something, a steady, paying job, she would appreciate his poetry even more. She sighed. No, that wasn't true. She appreciated and loved him and his anyway.

Her eyes, with part-reluctance, part-eagerness, settled on the first sheet of paper. She read the title and reflected on it... *Dance Again.* Then she was drawn again into the fluidity of Tony's poetic philosophy. It had been a long time since she last read any of his poems, and deliberately so... but now she began to peruse:...

Dance Again

People, spoil
Very slowly change
For worse
Soil becomes hard,
Abandon tenderness
Childlike humility
Lose the ability to change
Remain
Where we stopped
Slide into oblivion, proudly
Anxiously
You and I, know it, lost it

Search again
Youth of today
Take it, purely purely

Dive not into pools of rot
Spoil not the young
Soil not the truth

When did we become rigid
Forget how to dance
dance Inner music?

Our world has played a nasty trick on us
Tenderly, self, dance again
That inner dance
Before rigidity
Forever stills us.

Ada smiled and sighed and saw again her brother's heart and mind. Who he was. This was Tony. Forever still you. Suddenly it seemed to her as if she had just reunited with him after a long, much too long, separation. How could it have happened? When has they parted?

Then she lowered her eyes again, and read further, to know him all over again, her brother – *Young*.

Young

Heaven-born come the young
Happy, simple, free, humble, strong
Hearts full of wisdom
Naïve, ready to establish some perfect kingdom

We were young
 Never faltering, ever wandering with dream
With song

If the young shall rise anew
Then learn again to yearn, in deeds true.

She did not notice the woman sitting behind her, watching her intensely the whole time. Some people, they say, feel stares on the backs of the head. Ada was one such person, but not today. The poems had taken her away.

Behind her sat this woman, however, looking at her with a shocked question in her eyes, willing her to turn around. And when she didn't, the strange woman put her face briefly in her hands and wondered what to do. Ada was the last person she expected to see on this bus. She knew Ada, but Ada did not know her. She took long deep breaths to steady herself, and wondered what to do...

Ada meanwhile, completely absorbed in the poems in her hand, read on. The second had made her smile, but it was the third, The Touch, that she particularly liked. She had just now quickly read it once, had reflected shortly over it, and, lowering her eyes, read it again.

The Touch

Something different, something true,
Otherly, something new
Very small, something extra large,
Quietly in charge
Inside you
It is what you really are in your soul
You
Your start and your goal
Path, quest, your role
And it is, simply, you.

Someone touched her on her shoulder as she was thoughtfully reading that poem a third time. She turned around to see a young, very dark complexioned woman of about her own age peering questioningly into her face.

"Yes?" she asked, somewhat irritated.

"Sorry, I thought you were someone else. I'm sorry."

Ada relaxed and smiled at her, then turned back to the poems. But then she was tapped again on the shoulder.

Quizzically she turned her head round again, a slightly confused, even more irritated look on her face.

"Yes??"

The young woman hesitated again, then said:

"You look too much like someone I know –"

"I don't know you –"

"Yes, no, yes I know. Actually, to be frank, this person is a man."

"A man?"

"Yes."

"As you can see, I am a woman!"

"Please, don't be offended ... but ... is your name Ada?"

Ada's eyes focused sharply on the stranger. Her diction was clear and proper, she looked refined and was somewhat pretty, if not beautiful, with a small but african nose, a broad face and large, perceptive eyes. Her skin had that intense darkness that Blacks like to call 'black beauty'.

"I beg your pardon – How did? -"

"See, I have a friend called Tony whom you resemble to a high degree and he once told me that he has a twin sister called Ada. So I was just wondering... if..."

Ada softened; and realised that everybody around them was paying close attention to their conversation; thus, simultaneously, she became self-conscious and shy. – of course!, Tony! Where was her mind! – such thoughts too raced immediately through her mind., reflected in her eyes, those treacherous windows of hers.

"You know Tony?" she asked in a lowered, nicer voice.

The young woman's face suddenly lit up and she looked almost like a child. Radiant, naïve, open. Pure.

"Yes!" She struggled to keep her voice down. "My name is Ngozi. I knew him, er, in the university."

"I see," said Ada, feeling abruptly very uncomfortable. "Well, nice meeting you, Ngozi." She turned.

Ngozi, confused, raised her hand to tap Ada's shoulder a third time, hesitated, and then dropped it once more. Now she became aware also, for the first time, of the attention being paid her. She swept her eyes around and faces turned quickly away, conversations were struck up here and there, while a few understanding eyes surreptitiously melted friendly glances her way, then were gone too, and she was alone again...

Ada, in the seat in front, bent her head meanwhile into the sheets of paper in her hand, on the shopping bag on her lap, and, over and under, through and with the shudderings and other misadventures of the Molue, resolutely went into the assimilating of the fourth of the six poems – *earthly moments*...

Earthly Moments

Loneliness, heart
 Time breathes, in out
Endless time
 One foot ahead of the other
 The foot you left behind,

Drags
You lift it
Place it ahead of the other
With life, breathe, in out
Pain, unbearable, becomes bearable

Loneliness?
The earth, not our home
 We make it homely
But sooner, later
 We feel again
Loneliness?
Homesickness?
Loneliness, heart
And the loneliness won't leave your heart.

As Ngozi watched Ada reading some papers in front of her, she felt again the old loneliness creep back into her heart as thoughts of Tony came floating back, whisp by whisp, into her.

Oh, Tony.

Since they broke up, life had seemed quietly dismal to her. Empty, barren, not so much like night – which, when clear and lit up, is beautiful – as like a sunless, hueless, dreary day. A touch, a smile, a face, a voice... oh, how these could so make a difference in one's existence! Everything had changed after him. She needed a way out or in, she didn't know which. Going or coming? She felt trapped in an irresolute destiny. That was when she had started reading Sylvia Plath. Only there had she found a temporary home. And temporary had been long enough. Who needs forever when temporary can do the same job in a fraction of the time?

Why waste forever on the temporary? We will live on.

But, inspite of that, without Tony, the unfriendly world had become and remained even unfriendlier. She could take it, but it was still like a slap in the face. Harsh, stunning, demoralising. But sometimes it could be a clarion-call to action.

Like now!

She touched Ada resolutely a third time on the shoulder. Everybody around her secretly held their breath and guardedly watched this odd spectacle between these two young women.

Ada did not appear, for a second, to have felt the touch on her shoulder. Then she, with deliberation, turned her beautiful head to the man sitting to the right of Ngozi and spoke directly to him.

"Please, could we exchange seats."

Clearly the man was taken by surprise. His big eyes opened wider on his lean, black, bony face and he sputtered:

"Eh... er... okay."

Ada stood up, squeezed past the woman on her

right and, as she stood in the aisle, waiting for the man to slide past her, became – or rather, her legs became – the objects of general, if mixed, attraction.

Finally, though, the switch was concluded. The woman that had been to her right and thus on the edge of her former bench, had slipped into the position she had just vacated, in the middle, leaving the man to again be on the edge, like he had been in his former bench.

Ada, meanwhile, on this bench, indicated to Ngozi that she would like to sit in the middle, and Ngozi acquiesced. Side by side, they looked at each other.

Then, with a smile, they shook hands.

This indeed seemed, to the spectators around them, like an unexpected but pleasing dramatic finale to the live-show; an unconscious tension that had lain over each person broke and lifted and suddenly everybody burst into smiles as if a bubble had burst, a cue been given, a story found a worthy, happy ending. And everybody likes to know how the story ended. When it ends well, people smile.

Even the man who had taken the seat in front to make space for Ada beside Ngozi, turning just at the right moment with a bemused look on his face, also had to smile, although (which had prompted his turning around) the two fat-bosomed, big-bottomed women to his left were now forcing him to all but *perch* precariously with barely half of his buttocks on the tiny space they grudgingly allowed him on the very edge of the bench. Too late he had realised that his former seat was much more comfortable, but the damage had already been all but done. He thought immediately of asking for his former seat back, but you know women; the young lady would begin to talk upside-down jargon and by the time he managed to get his seat back, if at all, they would already be at their final destination.

Such were the thoughts going through his vexed mind when he turned round with that bemused look on his face of which I earlier spoke. When, however, he saw the two young women smiling handsomely and shaking hands, looking as though they would soon be hugging each other at any moment, although he had no idea why, the altruistic part of him was suddenly touched and, magnanimously contented, he turned round again with a transformed countenance and bore his fate on his new bench with a noble silence.

"So, Ngozi, what's your surname?"

Ngozi let her eyes roam again and again over Ada's features, marvelling at the incredible likeness they bore to Tony's. Twin-beauty.

"Eze-ebube's my last name," she replied. Before anything further could be said, however, her eyes darted down to the papers in Ada's hand, on her lap, and she recognised Tony's unmistakable hand-writing.

Ada saw the sudden breathdrawn look jump into Ngozi's eyes and automatically lowered her own eyes as well to the sheet that was now visible on top. On it, as title, boldly hand-printed, were the words SEEING THROUGH.

The two women looked at each other again and if there had been any clumsy last barriers between them, they crashed swiftly down now in the wake of the twin-look of deep, shared understanding that pulsated, in their eyes, from one to the other, and back again, on and on, into their hearts.

It was as though a million things had been spoken and shared, a million fears, a million experiences, a million thoughts of love and concept without number, had been settled, in that one look, after their simultaneous glancing at those words, SEEING THROUGH, in that hand-writing, and the knowledge and memory of innumerable loved poems, written in that hand, once read and stored away forever where hearts alone breathe.

A look in a million. No words were needed. The moment was fulfilled, their friendship sealed instantly as Ngozi gently lowered her eyes again to the poem in Ada's hand and, in a voice even gentler still than the look she'd just had in her eyes, began to read aloud, yet softly, audible to them two alone, heads locked together over poetry: "...

Seeing Through

Like bird I fly, fly out of sight
To the land of poetry, there I write
A poem for you, a poem for you
And a poem for me too

It is my work, it is my love
When I write I rise above
When I die, yes when I die
Nobody should weep Goodbye...

Because I leave, with every line
A part of me behind, undying
Weep not, o child, weep not, o child,
To simple words so mild...

Fly high with me, far beyond the sea,
To the worlds of art, song and poetry
And then beyond, into silent heights
A little closer to the Lights..."

With a sigh she was through.

And tears came a-calling softly gently tenderly. Tears for that thing, for which we often have no name, for which we are wont to cry when we cry. A little closer to the lights.

"So he still writes poems," Ngozi softly smiled, a tender look floating upon her features.

"It's in his blood. He will never stop."

"No, it really seems, not until he dies."

"Nay, not even then."

Ada and Ngozi here paused and searched each other's eyes.

"How is he?" asked Ngozi.

Ada shrugged.

"The same as always... I don't know... just himself, I guess..." She liked Ngozi's eyes and the look in them. Tender, deep, perceptive... strong. Feminine might. The bond, formed, was quickly cementing.

And memory was stirring...; she remembered... three, four years ago... Tony had spoken often of an Ngozi for a short space of time... Ngozi.

"You were..." she hesitated..., "close?"

Ngozi searched Ada's eyes for a cue, a thread to pick up and weave with, that she may construct adequately before Ada's inner gaze the nature, simplicity, the intricacy and the intense intimacy of the close relationship that she had shared, for one short sharp moment in time, with her twin-brother.

Finally she simply said:

"Yes – we were."

And again volumes were said, shared and mutually understood.

As though they feared to say anything further, their eyes went down again to the sheaves of paper in Ada's hands.

They had no idea of the kind of deep impression they were making on fellow passengers in this dreary bus. There was a similarity, mutually complementary, about them, and a wide gulf seemed to yawn between them and everybody around them. They were alone. They might have been on a hilltop, or on a lonely, deserted beach, or on a boat out at sea. So immersed had they suddenly, apparently yet unperceived by either, become in this shared moment, in this new union.

The Molue is the nastiest form of transport on Lagos roads, except for perhaps the motor-bikes, popularly called Okadas, nasty little metal-birds of the roads. But like a yellow cuboidal prison, this mighty monster of a bus absorbs human numbers like sponge water, clumsily sardines them and then imperils with every mile the lives and destinies of hundreds. Uncomfortable, dirty and dark on the inside, it is perhaps the last place many would expect to see two such pretty, neat young women immersed in poetry and poems that, like golden threads, spun the garment, upon tears, of a newly arising friendship.

But where there is life, there is hope.

Ada slipped open the sixth and final poem in the small collection –

YOUNG AGAIN –

Those were the words, that was the title.

"Were we ever young?"

"Did we ever age?"

Neither replied the other. Each had spoken for the other.

This last poem, for some reason, was italicised from first word to last. We shall be young one day again, younger than we ever were, young as ageless eternity. *YOUNG AGAIN.*

Young Again

It becomes simple
Crosses threshold
Mortality into immortality
Denseness into quickness
Old into new, call it young

The good become older
Grow younger
Younger and younger and younger
The better you
Lighter and truer
Younger grow

Let us all grow young again
Fill the Earth with laughter
With truth, with youth –

Ngozi looked into Ada's eyes and said:

"I want to see Tony again."

There was a pause. But did a spell break somewhere quietly? Or were we never there?

"Do you have a telephone?" Ngozi pressed, trying to interpret Ada's silence. It must mean something.

Suddenly Ada was taken aback.

A spell seemed indeed to abruptly lift itself off her and, in its place, her thinking cap, invisible on her head but visible in the sudden, guarded look in her eyes, treacherous windows, descended, full of fears and cleverness and innumerable bad memories, upon her. She was suddenly appalled at herself, and the last twenty minutes swiftly took on the aspect of a fairy-tale, a dream. Had it really happened? Who was this strange woman beside whom she was sitting, sharing the intimate poems of her brother with, like old friends. She experienced the sensation of having been swiftly disarmed and intruded upon, and even, oddly, deceived.

Her head moved back a fraction of a unit of precise measurement and re-appraised Ngozi with suspicious, half-friendly, half-unfriendly, unsure eyes. Like it was in the beginning. – Yes? *Who are you?*

The returning silence, cold and dividing, began to mature.

Ngozi suddenly understood Ada. She smiled tenderly. Into her handbag she reached, extracted a black, silver-capped pen and then a tiny slip of blue paper. Carefully she balanced the little paper on the side of her bag and, luckily, the bus was temporarily caught in a traffic-jam at Ijaiye. The type that Lagosians call the Standstill, in contradistinction to the Go-Slow and the Hold-up.

Quickly she wrote her name and telephone number down, then wordlessly handed it over to Ada.

"That's my office telephone number. Please tell him I said Hi." She smiled again, then turned her head forward; then turned back again, smiling even more disarmingly and added: "and, oh, by the way... Merry Christmas – one day in arrears."

"Same to you too..."

Ngozi had turned her face away. She didn't speak again. At the next bus-stop, Iyana-Meiran, she alighted from the bus and left a thoughtful Ada again without her presence, as it was in the beginning.

Chapter 2

...

Those who long shall grow.

The night was young. Young again. The moon, half-full, was banking all alone in the west of heaven, and there was, though no clouds were anywhere to be seen, a distant smell of rain. Sweet night rain, to bear our dreams softly down from heaven and wash our fears away; wash the old year away too and water the seeds of a new one. But the night, for now, was young and eager, eager to look into the homes and hearts of human beings, to know again their story.

Tony sighed – a deep sigh – and turned in for the night, wondering at the destiny that had returned Ngozi into his life.

He said goodnight to Ada and retired to his bedroom.

Quietly Ada watched her brother's back as he retreated into the bowels of the house in which they lived.

Softly the night crept into the house and touched, as it was touched by, the hearts, the hopes and the everyday history of the human race.

And deep into the night, between midnight and dawn, singing, singing, the rain fell softly down.

Chapter 3

...

Bright, exceptionally bright sunlight, shinning in through the wide open window of his bedroom mediated into Tony's still, relaxed form an increasing warmth until, nicely and freshly toasted, he awakened, with a dazed, wondering look on his face, into a new day.

The intensity of the rays, the glare, nay, the blare of this morning's sun startled him and, in that brief moment of attempted re-orientation, his dream receded into the depths of unconsciousness. Too late he tried to exit again his day-consciousness and retrieve the last moments of his fast-fading supra-earthly reality... to recapture, to retain, reclaim, to remember it... there was something that had just now been happening... but *what??* - - It was too late. The line had broken. He had lost it. Another buried dream.

He was again on the earth.

He sighed, rolled around, and sighed again. Wistfully. Everyday the same thing.

He rolled again, again he rolled, and sighed an even deeper sigh. He couldn't remember the dream, yet he could remember it ..., *how it felt*. It had been a particularly strong dream, this one. Near and far.

Yet, he knew, one day it would resurrect.

They always did.

Like Ngozi.

Dreams come back.

*

Tony was wide awake now. Faintly on his consciousness registered themselves the peripheral sounds of morning. Over the fence, the neighbour's pestle was hitting and rolling in the mortar with a quick rhythmic thumping, smooth but noisy, legacy of innumerable generations.

Tony purred like a cat and sighed again into the bright rays of the eager morning sun. Last night's surprise rain had tinged this morning's harmattan with the soothing touch of sweet wet bliss.

In the backyard, or from the boys' quarters, came the voice of the radio. Full of mixed opinions, it jumped from one topic to another like a mad and wise and, above all, delirious mind.

He listened a bit, but his interest soon slipped away from there and reluctantly focused on the issue of Ngozi. It was something he did not want to think about for the simple reason that he did not know what to think about it, *how* to handle it. So, yet again, like he had done the previous evening when Ada told him of her encounter with Ngozi, he rolled it carefully along the periphery of his thoughts for a few thinking seconds and then pushed it away and began to reflect instead on what 1999, only six days away now, would have to offer.

With this turn of his thoughts, suddenly he heard and perceived the sounds and smells of Yuletide again.

Christmas period in Lagos. No wonder the sun was so bright.

The radio had overcome its indecisiveness and settled down to singing Boney M Christmas songs. Songs that had accompanied him, Christmas after Christmas, from childhood into the harsh forests of adulthood. Songs of which he never tired.

There is no time like Christmas.

A knock on the door and Ada barged in, smelling of a happy, busy kitchen.

"Tah lah!" she called in a sing-song voice, half-skipping in and throwing her arms wide open the way she did almost every morning, as if to say "I'm here!"

And she said: "It's me again!"

"I perceive that it has not yet come to your notice that my door now swings, and most precariously so indeed, on only one hinge. It would be good to wonder why."

Ada burst out laughing.

"A mystery for Hercule Poirot," she replied between laughs.

"Even Hercule couldn't solve this one. Only you can

– with a simple *confession*; or, rather, *admission*."

"Confessions are for convicted felons. As a rule, one should only confess when all the evidence point irrefutably against one. As for admissions, I leave that to presidents and the like."

"You've changed o, you this woman! You now talk like a ring-leader."

She laughed again.

"Ring-leader of what?"

"Of the things that have ring-leaders. There are many of them. They are always getting caught every-day. Infact, most channels make it a point of duty, as is easy to verify, to show us arrested ring-leaders at least once every week – "

"And to showcase the unarrested ones at least once everyday," she added dryly.

"You can't blame them, when they have nothing else to show."

"Television is all about advertising –" she began, with the voice of a school-teacher.

"So they're advertising your fellow-ringleaders. You should be rejoicing. You people have taken over the world."

"Yes you should know. Aren't you the one always watching T.V.?"

Now he growled and jumped out of bed. He found himself laughing although she had just digged him again on a sore spot. He raised his clenched fists and began to bounce. She raised hers too and circled him.

"Ah, do you think it's all this silly bouncing? It's not like that, you have to be cool. Approach, let me teach you a painful lesson."

"I knew today would start with a morale-booster. I just never thought it would be this good – bestowing you with a swollen countenance. But let me apologise in advance –"

As he was talking she rushed forward with jabs.

"Wait wait wait –" he ran back and began to bounce again. "Hm, I'm *warning* you o! *What!* Are you laughing at me?? *Ok!*"

Now they began to shadow-box in earnest, but made no contact, pulling all punches just before impact, until he began to breathe harder and then leaned against a table.

A worried look immediately came into her eyes.

"How do you feel now? I thought you said –"

"Yes, I'm fine," he sighed. "I've recovered, but I'm still weak physically."

"You fall ill too often."

"That's my destiny."

They looked at each other without speaking, for a while. Then,

"I'm hungry. Ọkwọ Yuletide bonus is on the culinary way."

"Hm! Mchm!... " She made sounds not easy to spell and started to walk out of the room. "When Yuletide comes, you can ask him for your bonus! Me, I'm making my own *normal* breakfast. If you don't want to eat it, no problem … But don't let me catch you near the kitchen!"

He knew she was teasing. Something special was on the way.

"Ah-ah. Am I surprised?" he called after her through the door she'd left customarily ajar. "What else can one truly and honestly expect of a village-apparition…"

Her laughter floated back in, and he smiled too.

*

Somewhere else, Ngozi dressed up and went to work. Her mind was on Tony, wondering if he would call, hoping he would call, knowing, from memory and a deep understanding of him, that he might not, and why. And yet, wishing that he would surprise her all the same.

Tony did not call. – He came.

All of a sudden. She looked up and there he was, standing in front of her in her office in Anthony Village, a respectable, quietly opulent area of Lagos Mainland.

A little distance behind him, leafing in through the newly and quietly opened door, was the light of day, huskily harmattan. A car drove past further in the background, then another, as they smiled at one another. Her smile was open, his shy. She was amused, he was unsure. He took a step forward and shut the door.

Finally, she stood up. They looked at one another, unsure of what to do. Then she noticed how thin he was. A sharp, audible intake of breath, a full-throated hiss, was her first reaction. Then she came to him and touched his arm.

"Tony, you've lost weight."

What is the mystery of love?

"I've missed you," Tony said, speaking, like he so often did, without pausing to think, without ever even having once previously felt it. Since the resolution, years ago. Yet when he saw her, he remembered her again. And missed her. And had her. And was hers.

He let out his breath, slowly, deeply, and said it again:

"Wooow... I've missed you like *what!*"

"Like what?" she asked, smiling like a tease, re-membering and playing along in the word-game.

"Yeah, like what."

And they laughed, smiled, but did not embrace.

The weight of the years, somehow, lay yet upon them and between them. Memories of pain slowly arose. Tony saw it steal over her eyes like grey clouds across an open sky. He had hurt her. Deeply.

She had had her faults, some of them major pain-bringers. But in the end, it was he who had delivered the fatal blow. And she had not forgotten. It was in her eyes.

But had she forgiven?

"How did you know this place?" Ngozi asked, taking her hand off his arm and inching away almost imperceptibly and, thus, most perceptibly.

"Tony-magic," he smiled, twirling his fingers like a trickster.

They laughed again, partly to soften a heavy moment. Somewhere at the back of both their minds was the immediate understanding that this moment and how they handled it, and how it resolved itself, with or without their participation, would determine their future. Together or apart. Or what.

The undefined what.

Maybe because Yuletide had softened everybody. Maybe because of both their yesterdays. Maybe because of the manner and mood of this re-meeting. Maybe because they had never stopped caring. But, somehow, it was as though they had never parted. This was the moment in which they would meet or part.

Characteristic of Ngozi she wanted it settled at once. And it seemed to her as though she had been waiting and preparing for it all these years.

But characteristic of Tony he wanted to post-pone it again, like he did the last time. Imperceptibly. Like he was a master at doing.

Tony smiled and looked round her office. It had the

touch of beauty floating upon it, simple as it was, but he had the feeling that something was missing, without being able to place his finger on it.

There was an uncurtained window behind her seat, and, a toned contrast to the fluorescent be-lit room, again wafted in the light of day upon the tastefully designed, sturdy wooden office table, panelled-over with leather, colonised by but a tiny telephone on one side and nothing else. Tony noted that she still had that habit of being neat almost unto sparseness.

Her office was opened into by the door through which he'd just entered, behind which was a spacious business-centre.

He looked round her office again. There was a painting ... he ignored it.

She waited for his eyes to quit roaming, then trapped them again. For a second she thought she'd detected panic in there, but she couldn't be sure. His eyes, light brown and expressive, were amused and appraising as they settled on her one more time.

The moment, as though it had a will of its own, became now tender.

They embraced.

*

On his way home, Tony was very silent.

Outside the gate of his house, he felt the night-wind softly call, and he took out a sheet of paper from his back-pocket, and a pen, leaned against the wall and, whilst a bird sang somewhere near and somewhere far, like an ancient dream coming again, coming home, he wrote:

On This We Stand

Did you love me, did you not?
My, what a heart...
Did it break, broke it not?
I do not know –

Is it ending, is it beginning?
Hard to tell...
'Tis forever my love
Forever we are this –

This? What is this?
It is this:
Please be true to your heart forever.

Ada saw him from upstairs, leaning against the wall just at the edge of the gate, writing ... in the dark. How could he see what he was writing?

And he was always writing.

She heard a sparrow singing on a branch in front of the veranda. It was a lovely eternal song.

"Did you see her?" she asked him when he entered. She did not see any piece of paper in his hands. She could still hear the birdsong somewhere near and somewhere far and somewhere deep within her soul, a dream on the long walk home.

"Who?"

"Ngozi."

Tony searched for an evasive answer, then gave up. How did she know?

"Yes."

"And?"

"And what?"

"Forget it."

"She's travelling in six days' time."

"Where to?"

"Germany. University. Work. I don't know. She wasn't clear."

"Ouch."

"Yeah, double-ouch."

Later she said:

"The poems you gave me yesterday. They were nice."

"Hm."

"Ngozi read some too, on the bus."

"Hm."

"There's food in the kitchen."

"Thanks, I'm starved."

"She's a nice person; even almost special, I some-how think."

He was silent a while. Then he shook his head and said:

"It's complicated." - and walked into the kitchen.

Chapter 4

...

To understand the kind of person Folarin was, you have to understand that some people are beyond average understanding. They exist apart. Apart from that, it is also, to be frank, not easy generally to comprehend another human being. Each person is unique.

'Unique' was a word, therefore, of which Folarin was very proudly fond. He bathed in it and dissolved it in his blood. He made it part and parcel of himself. It was necessary that he never forgot: I am unique. Finally he had come to totally believe it, such that whereas he had once been always startled whenever he came across people who did not seem to notice or appreciate his uniqueness, now he merely looked down sadly on them, understanding their sorrowful limitations.

Even though it was the Christmas period, he was at work. He lived in Port Harcourt where he worked in the Information Technology section of Shell Petroleum Development Corporation. Today as he sat before his large-sized monitor he was in a good mood. He had just successfully installed a curious little software that had seemed, for a brief moment in time, like it would embarrass him before his colleagues. But – he smiled to himself – what can outwit the unique mind?

He took a deep bite into the doughnut he held triumphantly in his hand and then shook his head at it regretfully. Mournfully spoke he these words to it:

"*Eihn*… are you a doughnut? Ehh? Is this how a doughnut should taste? Oh, but shame on you…" and he dropped it sadly into the waste-bin by his black swivel-chair. These cafeteria people were really getting out of hand.

Simon, a colleague sitting in front of another monitor opposite Folarin in the large spacious room saw him drop it and asked:

"Man, Folarin, what's up? The doughnut…?"

Folarin waved a hand above his wisely nodding head and said in a slow, deliberate, audible voice:

"The doughnut is not unique."

"Oh dear," replied Simon in what sounded like a genuinely disturbed voice, "doesn't it deserved to be flushed down the toilet?"

"I couldn't inflict such a terrible punishment on an innocent toilet."

"Yes, you're right," said Simon gravely and turned back to his monitor.

Expansively, Folarin picked up the phone and, with the long nail pointing out of an index finger, began to delicately, luxuriantly punch in a telephone number.

From another corner of the office, Ibinabo, another co-worker, projected her voice at him. It was a friendly voice, but with a business-like quality in it:

"Folarin, I'm still being denied access." She was poised over her keyboard, a not at all amused look in the eyes that glared at an eighteen-inch colour monitor.

He glanced her way.

"Are you *sure* you're using the *right* Password?" In life, this Folarin now knew, success was always all about knowing and using the right Password.

The right Password. What else did one need? That was his new credo in life. Seek ye the right Password *first*, and all else shall be opened up to you. It was like magic. Only it was even better. Because, unlike magic, the right Password never failed.

"I used the same one I used before –" Ibinabo was speaking...

"Yah, hello?" He cut her off suddenly, addressing himself directly into the phone. But his eyes were still on her. She turned her gaze on him and he smiled and made a sign with his hand at her, telling her to be patient a while.

Then he swivelled fully into his desk and haunched into himself, over the phone.

On the other end of the line, Tony repeated:

"*He-llo...?*"

Folarin laughed into the mouthpiece.

"Was my Hello not unique enough for you to know immediately that it is I?"

"Ah, Folus-*gbosa*, my man!" charged an immediately lightened Tony's voice down the line, from Lagos to Port Harcourt, in the twinkling of an eye. E-speed.

"O boy, how far now?"

"Man, long time o!"

"Na wah."

"Is this your voice I'm hearing?"

"Unique voices are few..."

"This one that you're phoning me today, I'm sure it must be the harmattan that has lightened your mind."

"Harma*wetin?*"

"Harmattan, you know now. The season where *things dey happen*."

"Heh-heh, man, nothing like that here o."

"What do you mean? Nothing dey happen for your side?"

"No sign of harmattan and no sign of *things* around here, man. It's raining and the people are as hard as ever."

"Really? No sign at all?"

"*Naht*, men –"

"And we are generally enjoying some dreamsome, beautiful harmattan here."

"Good, let it stay there. We don't want it here at all. That guy! Harmattan!? Abegio!"

They both laughed. Folarin was playing with words.

"Well, since you don't want me," said Anthony Harmattan Chikezie, "I'll stay right here where people know how to appreciate better person." When the joked, they switched constantly between proper and pidgin English, like most Nigerians do.

They played a little longer with words and concepts, names and illusions, springing from harmattan to Christmas to uniqueness. Finally they felt sufficiently re-united and reconnected to settle into normal conversation.

"So how are you?" asked Folarin.

"So-so."

"What are you doing now?"

"Talking to you on the phone." A slight pause. Then:

"Man, you need to get on with your life." Folarin's voice was gentle and concerned. "You can't stay in your family house forever."

Silence.

Then a sigh.

"I just can't do anything yet. I can't."

"Why??"

"Folarin, believe me, when it's time, I'll be off."

"What of the school you were teaching in, in Ota?"

"Let's not talk about that now, please."

Folarin eased up a little.

"What you need is to come and spend some time in good old Port-Ha. You'll be cured in a jiffy."

Tony laughed.

"I'll think about it."

"Think well this time. Haven't you been thinking all this time? Brother, what use are thoughts when the password is not known?"

"I beg your pardon?"

"The Password, Tony. Look for the password."

"I have no idea what you are talking about."

"My point exactly."

"Precisely."

"I beg your pardon?"

"Ha ha, oh shut up, Folarin, I'm not in the mood right now."

They laughed.

"Anyway," said Folarin, "what's new?"

Folarin had a way of directing and controlling every conversation he had. Tony had learnt his own limitations with Folarin. But it was really always such fun talking to him. And deep within his heart, he had always believed Folarin to be his best, his only, friend.

"I saw Ngozi yesterday."

Dead silence. Followed by a whistle.

"Man. You two *again?*"

Now the conversation really became serious.

"She just popped up."

"So … what's the future like?"

"I wonder," said Tony. "How come you're working midway between Christmas and New Year?" He changed the subject directly.

For once, Folarin let him, understanding. He laughed and replied:

"You have to consider the uniqueness of things, Tony. If I were not here now, who would hold things in control? Think of the chaos that always ensues when I'm not around, I beseech you. For I am the man. The one all Nigerians have been waiting f –"

"Will you shut up, you green-eyed gold-digger!"

"Ha!... Any problem?"

"On the contrary."

They both burst out laughing again. Laughter was followed by speech. Speech was followed by laughter. Thus did they conduct their conversation.

Finally, Folarin said:

"I just called to say hello, since you never call. No, no, don't excuse yourself, just count yourself amongst the fortunate few that occupy the unique heart of the F. Take care, I've got to get back to work. My unique mind is again in demand. Don't forget to say Hi to Ngozi for me, good friend."

"... Merry Christmas, man..." said Tony in a gentle voice, and replaced.

Warmth. Yes, that too.

*

Tony remained sitted, staring at the ceiling, long into the time after the end of the conversation with his friend. Many, contradictory, emotions tearing him apart.

And he was trying to understand himself.

He couldn't.

He could write. He could touch people's hearts. He could write out what was in himself, but he did not know himself. Not at all.

He did not know why he had dropped out of university, why he just could not function there or go through it. He did not know why he couldn't hold a steady, paying job. He did not know why, inspite of loving so many women, he always managed to avoid every consummate intimate relationship. He did not know why he was the way he was. Why he had no fear of being a societal outcast. Why he could sometimes take so much crap from empty-headed, little-hearted people. Why he did not feel ashamed of himself whenever he saw or heard of his mates 'getting ahead' in 'life'. Often he felt a pressure, it was true, but it never broke him. Like a wave, it rose… it fell. And left the sea of his soul again, rocking, rocking, perpetually rocking, a poet…

Tony Harmattan Chikezie was a poet.

All he could do. All he loved doing. All he would do. Was write, compose and mediate poetry.

Is that so hard for people to understand?, he often thought. I am an artist.

*

"That's just how he is," said Ngozi to Ada as they sat

facing one another over her desk in her office.

"But this is *Nigeria*. You can behave like that Away, if you like, and get away with it. But *not* in Nigeria! You will become the object of people's pity or laughter or scorn even as you rot away in poverty. A 'poetic life', or whatever it is, is for rich white people. A young, *jobless*, black man like him should be securing his future and his name. Why can't he see that? Okay, look now: nobody wants to help him publish it. Scattered him, he doesn't even know how to go about it! Is that the way forward? I've told him: *go back to school, get a degree, get a job, become SOMEBODY!* Then everybody will be eager to buy your poetry. Even if they don't read it, which is even better. Infact, they prefer to buy the ones they won't read. It's more convenient. And safer for the poet too. Once people begin to read your works, next thing they'll be crucifying you. Life is actually easy, but my poor brother has not understood the Way. The crooked way that leads straight to comfort. And please nobody should quote me any Khalil Gibran on comfort!"

Ngozi quietly watched Ada as she agitatedly complained, arguing with nobody except maybe herownself, going on and on as though unable to stop. When she wanted to stress a point she would arch her back, lift her head and then thrust her face forward, her eyes narrowing into near-slits. It wasn't ugly on her, no. It leant a sudden intensification to her already so powerful aura and accentuated her striking dark beauty. – This face – in *this* moment – ought to be reproduced on canvas by a passionate painter, was the chance thought that flashed through Ngozi's mind.

But she was also amused, amused by the moment. She understood Tony so well and had long come to accept him for what he was. But here was his own twin-sister who, though she apparently loved his poetry, couldn't really fathom or countenance his ways. Yet, Ngozi understood and sought for a way out.

"The way I see him, he's just hibernating. He's going through an early winter in his life, a deep, serious harmattan..."

They both smiled.

"He's undergoing some fundamental changes in his soul. It won't last forever."

Outside were the sights and sounds of Anthony Village. It was quiet. It didn't really feel like Christmas.

"This Christmas is not like Christmas," said Ada abruptly, changing the subject.

"Christmas stopped being like Christmas long ago. There's maybe a lot of music, noise, jovity... but no Christmas."

"Yeah..." Ada nodded and the two women, in that moment, were again of one mind.

"This year has been a strange one, though," said Ngozi, making conversation.

"Strange? How?"

"For the country, I mean," said Ngozi quickly, "first Abacha died, then Abiola, now Obasanjo – who was in jail – is gunning for the presidency."

"Nothing is strange in Nigeria."

"You know: strangely enough, you're right."

"Nigeria is the country that never was."

"Ha-ha, never was *what?*"

"Oh, always was everything; yet never was."

Ngozi gazed reflectively at Ada.

"You know you're deep?"

"I have to be, to bury all my sorrows in."

Ngozi sighed again, her almost plain but curiously attractive dark-complexioned face softening as she observed the twin features and feminine reflection of Tony. Ada had the same beautiful countenance of her brother's. But they were panning out to be very different inwardly.

"Do you have lots of sorrows?"

"We all do, don't we?"

"Oh, Sorrow, Sorrow, Sorrow. Why plaguest thou us so?"

The two women, chuckling, regarded one another with something like surprise. The speed with which they had become one, and the intensity – yet naturalness – of this union, was for both still a wonder.

After parting in the bus two days earlier, each had found, to her surprise, that she badly wanted to see and talk with the other again.

"Come, tell me: how did you even know or find this place?" asked Ngozi. "I only gave you my phone number, and I don't remember this place being listed on any directory."

"I got the address and route-description from Tony this morning."

"And how did he get it? It's not in any directory that I know of."

Ada twirled slim, well-manicured fingers like a magician's assistant, smiled and whispered confidentially:

"Tony-magic."

Ngozi shook her head incredulously, rocking with laughter.

"One minute, I'm beginning to think that both of you are exact opposites, the next you are acting exactly like him!"

"Now, how many times have I heard that in my life!"

They were silent awhile. Ngozi offered Ada another drink, Ada declined. Ngozi then popped open for herself a second soft-drink bottle which she'd just extracted from the little fridge to her left. Above the fridge was a beautiful painting of a mountain growing out of a lake, arising majestically from the depths of water, under the fiercely possessive gaze of a fierily amber sun whose blaze touched and permeated everything. The parting white waves were red. The dark mountain was red and crowned with the stern, mysterious, mysteriously beautiful face of a gigantic lady of the sea, queen of the mountainpeak... Ada contemplated her powerful dual-personality as she gazed again, like she had done when she'd first entered, in impressed awe at the large-sized painting on the wall, brightly illumined by the twin fluorescent tubes on the ceiling.

"This painting must have been done by a European! And a european male, at that. It bears the mark of both."

Ngozi shook her head, surprised that Ada should have judged so incorrectly.

"No; it was done by a Nigerian – "

"Really?! Wow! We have artists in this country o!"

"We have everything in Nigeria. It's on record."

Ada laughed.

"How much did he sell it?" she asked.

"I believe the artist who did it wasn't a he, it was a woman – "

"Truly?"

"Yes. Selling price ... er ... mm, well, over eighty thousand."

"What!" Ada appraised Ngozi again with a question in her eyes.

"Don't look at me that way! I didn't buy it."

Ada relaxed visibly.

"So what's it doing hanging in your office?"

"My office indeed! My boss is on Christmas hols. I'm just holding fort temporarily for him. He'll be back in a few days."

Many things registered in Ada's consciousness. She heard what the words said and she heard what the voice said, and she heard some thing unspoken.

She turned from the red painting and, leaning back in her seat, appraised Ngozi again, but this time with a quite different look in her eyes.

She went for the kill.

"Are you second in command after the boss?"

Ngozi winced. *Second in command*. Sounded like a war.

"Mm... actually, no..."

"He, your boss, apparently has great confidence in you then."

The chess game started.

"Sort of. There was no-one else to sit in for him in his absence."

"I thought I saw a lot of workers in the outer office. Or have you worked here that long?"

Ngozi couldn't believe Ada's audacity. Two days earlier, on the bus, she had also noted her directness, somewhat impolite, perpetrated with such candid, intelligent eyes that it left little psychological room for manoeuvre. Now here she was, suddenly asking her in no mistakable terms if she was having an affair with Tanko.

Was she supposed to feel guilty? She ran straight into the offensive.

"Long enough to become close enough," she smiled, levelling amused steely eyes at Ada the interrogator, the unsettler. Unsettler unsettled. Game kaput.

"Yes, time and space operate together, don't they?" Ada could not immediately figure out why she felt betrayed all of a sudden. It was very foolish, thought she, and tried to quickly overcome it. Strange, the things we suddenly sometimes unexpectedly feel under given conditions, how ever absurd.

Ngozi, perceptive as a sensitive plant, adroitly watched Ada battling with herself, again reading her new friend with amazing ease. Liking her, loving her, reaching out to her.

"Did you tell Tony?" Ada asked Ngozi.

Ngozi nodded.

Ada couldn't help it. She smiled. She felt his pain, yet she smiled at the unbelievability of Ngozi.

"You *told* him about..."

"Tanko."

"*Kai*. What did he say?"

Ngozi shook her head at the unbelievabilty of Tony.

"He gave me – seriously – advice on how not to scare Tanko away."

"What!" Ngozi's eyes opened wide and she burst into laughter.

"Your brother is beyond my comprehension!" said

Ada, then, after the laughter, said one word, simply:

"Ngozi…"

"Yes…?"

For the next few minutes they didn't speak. The A/C hummed coolly, unperturbed by their presence.

"It's like I've always known you," one of them said.

"Same here," replied the other.

Ada got up to go. Her eyes flickered to the powerful red painting on the wall for a second, then she looked at Ngozi and asked gently:

"Did you scare Tony away?"

"When? Yesterday, or four years ago?"

"Ever?"

Ada saw Ngozi really unsure for the first time today.

"I don't know … Tony. Sometimes he's a closed book."

They stood facing each other.

Circles of Experiencing

...
Oh dear,
She's back, again
Is she?
How deep
Within?
Sea
All these deep things in our hearts,
Oh dear
What is love?

One surprising day
It will find its end
Its start
Walk again
Circle of one love...

Did she ever go?
I'm there again –

Chapter 5

. . .

Ada sat down again and, to her great surprise, Ngozi felt a giant wave of joy and relief wash through her. It must have shown on her face.

Because Ada half-pointed at her, smiled and said:

"You don't want me to go, eh?"

Ngozi laughed, almost giggled infact like a shy girl whose secret wish, without being expressed, has been deduced and granted immediately.

"I'll soon be travelling. I want to know you very well before I go. I feel it almost like a need."

"Na wah o – " again they laughed. As a rule they laughed a lot. But together it felt extra special. They felt almost shy in the wake of the quality of happiness they were feeling. Like soul-sisters.

Ada glanced at the A/C.

Ngozi noted it, asked:

"Are you cold?"

"For the past fifteen minutes I've been freezing. A/C in harmattan. O-girl you theque o."

"I'm practising for Europe." They both laughed.

Ngozi switched the air-conditioning unit off. Without complaining, it coolly held its peace.

A new mood had overtaken this moment. Gently friendly.

"And *can* you speak german, if I may ask?" Ada had relaxed more unguardedly into the rather half-comfortable, posh, plush office-chair.

"Yes, I learnt it at the Goethe Institute." Ngozi sipped at her drink as she spoke.

"And what's that?" Ada inquired with the attentive eyes of one who's always gathering new information.

"The german cultural centre. It's in V.I.. Opposite 1004. They teach people, who wish to learn it, how to speak their language."

"Na wah o. Everybody is teaching Nigerians foreign languages these days."

"We ourselves – are we not foreigners?"

"To be frank, there are very few indigenous Nigerians left."

"*Indigenous Nigerian?* What's that?"

"I've forgotten. They taught me in secondary school, but it has slipped my mind now. But if you give me a few minutes, I'm sure I'll remember."

"Forget it."

"Don't be tautological..." laughed Ada.

"Tautology does not apply to Nigeria. No matter how many times one says it, it's never stale or repetitious."

They both laughed. A Non-Nigerian might wonder

why they spoke so badly about their country, whereas in their minds they were not speaking badly about her at all, just making jest *with* her, telling her in an upside down way that they loved the hell out of her.

"You know, Nigeria is a great country o."

"Are you just knowing that one now? It's on record. Nigeria is the only country in her own category. We are special."

"Is that why you're going to Germany?"

"No, not at all. I know I'll miss Naija!"

"Yes. Many Nigerians who go abroad get missing..."

Ngozi laughed and said:

"I thought that was the whole idea."

Ada cocked her head and asked quietly:

"Is that *your* idea, Ngozi?"

Ngozi answered with an honest shrug:

"No, I'm not that type – I think."

"I know you're not. But someone will miss you here."

That statement, ambiguous as it was, brought them to a touchy center.

"How long has he been ill?" asked Ngozi, leaning forward and placing both her fore-arms on the soft leather surface of the table. Her eyes were divided in their content. When she had first seen Ada on the bus and then subsequently obtained the confirmation that she was Tony's sister, she had impulsively given her her number along with the uttered wish to see him again. Tanko had flown from her mind then. Even the old hurting had been temporarily forgotten. Instead, a consciousness deeper than daily thoughts had awakened in her. Consciousness of a buried need. An unanswered question.

Now she had no control over what was beginning to happen all over her heart again. She was beginning, once again, to care. And it made her nervous.

"He's alright now," replied Ada, but without much enthusiasm. "But I was very scared…. I'm still not fully rid of my fear either."

"Malaria?"

"Malaria… typhoid… - I don't know the difference anymore. He's always succumbing to one or the other."

"Why? He wasn't like that in Uni."

Ada shrugged. Both of them tried not to think the fatal thought. It couldn't be. But he had lost so much weight. What else could it be? Afterall, this was the nineties, hey, this was the turn of a new millennium.

AIDS is real.

"You know, I don't believe that thing about him needing a university degree. I really don't believe it at all."

There was a fierceness in Ngozi's voice, and an ideological ring therein too, that startled Ada. Obviously, Ngozi was considering the matter on a very different plane entirely, whereas she, his sister, was only thinking of the earthly pragmatic, which wasn't in her opinion a very bad thing to think about. And she didn't want her brother to be a guinea-pig.

"Really??" she said, noting also, vaguely, gratefully, that the subject had been changed.

"Yes, indeed."

"Well, that's easy for you to say," Ada retorted bitterly, "you're a graduate; you have a degree. You can hold your head up high anywhere, anytime, no matter what. Tony doesn't have the protection we have!"

But Ngozi shook her head vigorously, causing her short, beaded braids to sway and swish, knocking a little, over her introspective countenance.

"That's all hogwash, Ada. A man is a man, no matter what. And Tony is a man."

There was a sudden loud knock on the door, shattering the tense magic of the moment, and a woman with improperly applied make-up looked into the office.

"Yes?" asked Ngozi in a voice polite, friendly and terse all at once, pinning her at the door with her eyes.

"It's the photocopying machine, Ma. It has started again." Her voice was heavy and grating.

"Which one?"

"That one that spoiled before. It has started again this morning, now now."

"Started *working?*"

"Ah, no o. Started spoiling."

"Call me Dele."

"Yes, Ma." The door clicked shut.

Ada raised her eyebrows at Ngozi.

"*Ma??*"

Ngozi shrugged, and tried to do it non-chalantly.

"I think they think we're going to get married."

"You and the boss?"

"Yes – Tanko and I."

Ada looked away from Ngozi's gentle eyes for a moment and abstractly brushed away nothing from the sleeve of her green soft-collared linen blouse.

Then she asked, glancing back at Ngozi:

"Are you?"

Ngozi shook her head. A moment later she said, smiled:

"Why, Ada, but you looked so relieved." – –

"Tell me, Ngozi: do you love Tony? Do you *want* him? What's up between you two? Tell me, do, please. He's my twin, and friend, ...and you... I don't know... my heart likes and trusts you."

"And your mind?" Ngozi enquired, watching Ada without seeming to do so, putting off her answer.

Ada thought about that a while, then changed her line of thought, then said:

"My head too, but – "

A sudden, loud knock sounded and a small-sized young man, definitely not past his mid-twenties, strutted in as though he owned the place. Over rather solid sneakers he had on a pair of pale blue jeans and over them a black T-shirt on which, clearly printed, were the words AREA BOY?

"Ngọ, what's up?" he said casually to Ngozi.

Ada, turning back to Ngozi, caught, just before it vanished, the overpowering look of contempt in her eyes.

It was replaced by cold anger.

"Dele," she said softly... "You are sacked!"

Whatever response he had expected, it wasn't this. He seemed to double back on his stride, tripping almost.

"Ah-ah! *What! Whaaat?!*"

The unexpected clash of anger, like leaden, erupting waves, took Ada's breath away. She shifted, without even first consciously willing it, out of the line of fire, and watched, powerless to do aught else.

There was a war of wills for a few moments, buffeted by the roaring of total silence. –

Dele wilted. Or did he? The defiant look he'd just had on his face, as well as the cocky one with which he'd entered, remnants of which had somehow still managed to cling on even in the wake of her sudden offensive, were both wiped off his features with prompt alacrity, to be supplanted, after a period of vacuum-like uncertainty, by a cunningly guarded one.

"You know I was just joking." He spoke good english, only slighted accented, not really an ethnic-based accent, simply a 'Lagos' accent, quite similar to hers.

They were about the same age, working in the same establishment. But to Ngozi's mind, that was as far as the equality went. Besides, she was a firm non-believer in the equality of the sexes. Women were higher. Fullstop.

"*I'm not your mate, Dele,*" she said to him with cutting deliberation. It was a statement calculated to cause injury, to wound deeply, and she saw, in his eyes, that it had more than achieved its objective. And, like a boxer on top of an opponent, she followed up: "And you know that I can *fire* you, if I so wish. You are beneath me."

She paused again to let him experience the pain. Then, like a colonial master after re-conquering a troublesome tribe, laid down her unnegotiable terms of settlement:

"If you *ever* enter *my office* again before I say EN-TER..., or ever *ever* refer to me in any other way than *Miss Eze-ebube*..., young man, I shall rob you of your means of livelihood! *Do I make myself clear enough?!* - - - I'm certain I do. – Now, go and assess that trouble-some photocopying machine, and then report back to me at once. I want to know exactly what's wrong with it and how much it'll cost to fix it. Immediately."

Somehow, they all three must have sensed that she had gone much too far. And Dele was afterall more than a man, he was also a human being. Yet still a man. He could only take so much from a colleague. From a woman. This was Dele. He glanced sideways into Ada's eyes and knew that she knew that Ngozi had gone too far, but was watching him to see what he would do. I think it was her presence there that did it. That undid it all. And Dele, looking back later on this moment, could only feel deep satisfaction. Two wrongs, three wrongs, four wrongs, they all make a perfect right; if executed firmly.

Dele marched up to the table and, over it, leaned forward slightly and with the open palm of his right hand whacked Ngozi hard, across the side of her face. It rocked her head, and her braids, in wild disharmony, slapped noisily all over her countenance. In Nigeria, such a slap is termed a dirty slap.

Two pairs of eyes, Ada's and Ngozi's, jerked open *wide!*

Coolly, mechanically, he slapped her again, solidly, with the back of his hand, on the other cheek. Blood trickled out of her nose. Another dirty slap. There was violent anger in his eyes, increased, not decreased, it seemed, curiously, by the two blows he'd just struck his opponent. The atmosphere was charged. Nay. CHARGED. Dele lips curled into a semi-smile as he saw the shocked alarm jump into Ngozi's eyes.

The artist, whoever she was, that had wrought the red painting pulsating down on this confrontation now, would perhaps not ever have found a worthier human interpretation, in living drama, of the fiery explosive powerfulness encapsulated by her work of art – and happening right in front of it too, like the changed yet *accurate* reflections of images upon the laughing surface of a magic-mirror-of-truth-and-transformation. *Show me your face*, sayeth the mirror, *and I'll show you your heart!*

And into this picture Ada rose. The spectator entered the show. The viewer slid into the t.v. screen. Suddenly the impassive critic appeared inside the very painting under appraisal, to personally change the offensive feature of the art-work, substituting clear action for misinterpretable words.

Ada was on her feet beside Dele, and her one slap outsounded the two he'd landed on both cheeks of Ngozi. It was so loud and sounded so painful and – what is more – soo overwhelmingly dirty, *filthy*, that it was not only heard outside, but also brought worried, puzzled people rushing into the office.

When they opened the door, they saw Ada, tall, brown, slim and overpoweringly beautiful, towering over Dele who had the look of a fast-deflating balloon, his fingers raised unto slight contact with his cheek, a look of wild confusion in his eyes ... and sitting on the boss's chair across the table was a stunned Ngozi, frozen in multi-dimensional shock.

Then Dele awoke, awoke again. And his victory was a smile. A Lagos smile. A dirty smile. He was untouched.

The silent A/C offered no comment, and the red painting on the wall totally dominated proceedings, looking down with aloof power, through the mysterious, mysteriously driving eyes of the sun-crowned mountain-lady of the lake, upon its reflection.

And, like always, its painter was its victim.

Like always.

*

It was an hour later.

Dele was gone. Permanently temporarily.

The business center was at work again. The six people on duty in the outer office today could hardly settle back into calm work. It had already been difficult before, what with the festive mood and all. And now this! Wow, what a Christmas bonus!

Opinions, as is characteristic with them, were many, mixed and varied. Nothing was fixed.

"Dele for kill dat small girl! *Mchm!* Na him make mistake." This was whispered menacingly by the girl who had reported the faulty photocopying machine to Ngozi. Her improperly a-smeared make-up hadn't yet slid into harmony with convention or beauty.

Another woman, older, more refined, said coolly:

"She will fall into my trap *one day.*" Compared to the emotional ejaculation of the first woman, this one was frightening in its cool, freezing equanimity. Obviously there was something under it. Some unspoken but deep grudge, waiting to do damage.

"She now brings her friends here to also insult us; imagine." It was the same quietly bitter woman, nursing silent hatred. Having said her piece she turned to a customer who was just walking in.

Miss Improperly-applied-Make-up repeated her opinion, slightly remixed:

"Why Dele no *kukuma* kill am sef? Eihn? Abi şe him dey fear dat *pikin?* Di way some men dey do dey too dey surprise me atynes o! Me I weak."

This must have struck a glancing blow, if nothing else, on the ego of one of the four men – the rest of the workers there then – for he pointed at her with a pencil and growled in a half-serious voice:

"Youu no get hand? Why you never go slap Ngozi since, nau? Even sef, wetin she do una? Na so-so provoke provoke dat Dele boy don dey provoke everybody here since. Na him don find today di tin wey him don dey find since wey him begin to dey work here."

With this utterance the dividing line began to form and then to thicken. The speaker had assumed that in a way he was speaking for all the men here, but another man there who had no liking at all for the speaker, waited for him to finish his short rally and then pounced on him:

"Are you not a graduate? Eh?" He spoke evenly, deliberately. "Yet *every* time you open your mouth, the only thing that staggers out is *Pidgin!* Is that not perhaps why you hate Dele? Because he's always correcting you *for your own benefit?!* Can't you speak any english at all? I mean, what on earth was the purpose of the sixteen years of school you wasted money on if you can't even speak english? – eh, tell me. *Illiterate!*"

The first man's eyes nigh on popped out, his eyelids reached for his already receding hair-line.

Clearly, a new dimension had been herewith introduced to the argument. More, therefore, would most probably definitely be quickly and duly added like in a well-rehearsed stage-drama. Because, of course, there had always been running battles between different persons here, like everywhere else. The only thing ever needed was an event to trigger it off and, soon, everybody would settle into his and her own long-accepted camp-formation, all roles fully practised. In real life, actors don't forget their lines. That only happens on stage.

Tony had sensed the suppressed over-excitement as soon as he'd entered, had heard Ngozi's name mentioned and had listened carefully, something he did not often do.

The argument escalated. Tony couldn't figure out what it was about.

He turned to the woman facing him and said:

"Madam is expecting me," and moved past her. It was a trick he had learned years ago. Don't ask. Take. Don't request. Inform. The world is yours – under the right conditions. And when those conditions are not there, then create them. No one else will do it for you, brother.

He caught the eye of a man he'd met here the day before and nodded briefly at him as he moved straight towards the door at the centre of the rear wall. The boss's office.

He opened it and entered, without knocking. But just before he did so he looked back on the suddenly hushed room. Six pairs of eyes were on him. It was too much for him. He turned away quickly, opened the door and hurried in, shutting it firmly behind him again.

The two women welcomed their man in solemnly.

The battle, the humiliation, the victory, the loss, had forged of them one quietly silent, powerful, uniform whole.

Tony experienced an odd sensation, which he could not immediately define, as his eyes fell on them. Later, in the night, just before he dozed off, he got the answer to the question that arose at this moment somewhere deep within him. It was as though he were seeing not two persons, but one Siamese, coolly regarding an outsider from the four fierily different cardinal points of view offered by two pairs of angry eyes and resolved within the flaming embers of one primeval, gigantic heart.

They were one.

"Is anything the matter?" he asked, standing un-comfortably before the closed door, in reply to the Siamese's low-keyed "Welcome". What was up in this establishment? First in the outer office, and now here.

"No," it said, "everything is fine."

But that was as far as it got. It was then as though scales suddenly dropped from their eyes and they re-alised who was standing at the door.

"Ah, Tony!" it was Ada. "Do you know what hap-pened?!" She was already moving towards him. She took his hand.

But he looked not at his twin-sister, but at Ngozi sitting at the table.

"What happened?" he asked softly.

"One *idiot-youngman* actually *slapped* Ngozi..." Ada stopped abruptly as she saw the look in his eyes. She gazed back at Ngozi and then turned to him again.

He and Ngozi were staring straight into each oth-er's eyes.

"Where is he?" Tony asked, softly.

Ngozi was still not speaking. Her eyes were locked on his, his on hers. They appeared chained to one an-other.

"He's gone," said Ada more than a little hurriedly, her voice changing as she looked anxiously from Tony to Ngozi and over again.

The tension was incredible.

What kind of tension was this? It baffled and bothered Ada.

She slipped her hand away from around his and took a little step to the side, and watched, powerless to do ought else.

Once again she was the spectator.

Once again, Ngozi and a man were locked, will on will, but whereas the first time had been a fight,... this one was...

What?

Ada had no idea. It felt like a battle, a war, but that made no sense.

What then could it be, this vibration so thick, so tense, so dense?

Tony moved towards Ngozi, tense. Ngozi got up from her seat. They might have been re-playing a well-rehearsed script.

Suddenly, without knowing why, Ada felt afraid.

As the two of them met, by the table, beneath the red-painting, Ada turned her face away. And prayed to God.

Why, she didn't know.

Chapter 6

...

After Ada had gone, Ngozi locked the door of the office and returned to the boss's chair. Their eyes, as they loved doing, met again.

There was something not right about the office, but Tony still couldn't put his finger on it. It wasn't a very big office. Apart from the medium-sized tables, the two chairs and the little refrigerator, there was a small, low filing cabinet against the wall beside the door and nothing else. The white walls and the fluorescent lights gave to – and yet, in their eager unnaturalness, simultaneously took away from – the place an appearance of light and space, and the only form of decoration was the red painting on the wall, so terribly powerful that it alone seemed to rule the room.

Yesterday, Tony had pretended not to see it. But today felt different and the charge accentuated the presence of the painting.

They both knew why he didn't want to acknowledge it.

After Ngozi sat down, Tony stood up.

He walked silently around the table, towards her.

Her breath caught silently, inaudibly, visibly, in her throat. The tension was growing, mounting. His eyes were on her. The pulse-beat in her throat increased geometrically, immediately.

He walked past her and turned on the A/C on the wall. Gently it began to hum, a soft, hushed accompaniment to this subtle drama.

She felt his presence behind her swivel-chair.

He took a short step to her left, bent down, opened the fridge and brought out a bottle of bitter lemon. His footsteps as he walked back to his chair were silent on the worn but dampening carpet.

Ngozi felt her breath softly ooze out of her as she watched him put the bottle in the back of his mouth and carefully, steadily uncork it with his troublesome molars.

"You ought have stopped doing that by now," she said with forced formality, a minute tremble in her voice, "you know you have a temperamental dentition."

Tony took a long gurgling swig that rid the green bottle of half its contents. He smiled innocently, like a boy. They both had innocent smiles.

Tony pointed to the red painting and said:

"You've improved ... but you haven't changed. If anything, you've become even more intense." He nodded. "But you've improved."

There was a moment of silence, then he added:

"Is that it?" pointing again to the painting.

"That's what became of it."

"Everything is there – all the anger."

That was it. He had said it. He had acknowledged it. Such a small statement, yet everything.

What would come next? An approaching or a receding? Or would she pursue the point? Or expect it to be self-explanatory? What of him? *What* did he want? There is nothing more irritating than when the most obvious thing bears a face obscure, thus that one doesn't know what to say or how to say it or whether to say anything at all.

Is silence not the best answer, not for fools alone, but even more so for the wise?

Yet silence it is, above all, that misses always, more painfully than words can say, the golden opportunity to say the right word. Silence, too, misses the point.

Ngozi shrugged, but kept her eyes on him. Those big, perceptive eyes of hers.

He got up again, turned and walked to the door. The key was still in the keyhole. He turned it, unlocking the door.

He returned to his seat.

Like a cloud broken up by fierce winds, the tension dispersed and Tony and Ngozi smiled. It was always that way with them. Things happened suddenly, immediately, or not at all. Or never at all.

*

Tanko turned his car out of Ikorodu road into Anthony Village. The short road ended in another slightly longer one. He turned left, then right again and finally stopped but a few steps away from his Business-centre and office.

The sun was hot as he stepped out of the car, wearing a short-sleeved tie-and-dye over light, blue trousers. A handsome moustache curved above his full, dark lips and the hot rays of the dry sun burned down on his squinting face.

He locked the door and was about to walk to his establishment when a voice called him from behind. He turned.

It was Dimeji, a casual acquaintant and drinking buddy from the area. Dimeji was sometimes broke and always friendly, a clever mix.

"Ah, brother. Tanko, you're back?" he asked, looking up into the sharp, watchful eyes of Tanko.

"Yeah, Dimeji. Brother, how now? You know I only went to visit my sick mother. But she's not as ill as I, through her messenger, was given to believe. Hm, she's not even ill at all. You know how women operate."

"Abi, brother don't I know...hm! *Women?!*" Dimeji turned down the corners of his lips satirically, laughed derisively and hissed derogatorily. His entire aspect was soaked in sarcasm. Then, remembering suddenly that the woman in question was Tanko's mother, he quickly changed the expression on his face to a tired one and wisely executed a philosophical shrug of the shoulders, coughed lightly and said:

"Hhmm."

Tanko was watching him carefully as he did all this. Dimeji turned his face away as though he'd just seen something by the side.

At that moment Ada walked out of Business First, Tanko's business centre a few steps further down, on the other side of the road. Dimeji saw her and Tanko, seeing the new look in his Dimeji's eyes, turned his head that way too. His breath caught in his throat.

From instinct, Ada had learned to be aware of the turn of a man's head or even just eyes in her direction. As a rule, she never gave them her eye, but maybe because her thoughts were still on Ngozi and Tony back in the office, she without thinking automatically turned her head to where the attention was coming from.

Her eyes were caught by a big, moustached man, his eyes absorbed in her body, then her eyes. She experienced a light shock work its way briefly but deeply through her body. She saw a loneliness, a childlike need, but also an earth-grounded strength in his eyes that threatened to get her thoughts going. But she recovered swiftly and, returning his stare, she swallowed his eyes with hers for a moment, in that way which she knew disoriented men, then turned her face away and walked off.

Tanko watched the long legs striding away beneath gently swaying hips.

The two men were silent a while.

When they looked again at one another, there was a slight look of guilt, of minor complicity, even naughty camaraderie, in their eyes and, for this moment, they felt essentially united. So they smiled, said Brother, and began to chatter away on other topics, until finally Dimeji was able to wean a few hundred naira off Tanko, as had been his original intention, and as Tanko had fully suspected.

*

Ngozi and Tony were locked together in a deep look. Eyeball to eyeball. They were not speaking, just looking at one another.

Oddly, there was a sense of danger in the air. Tony could feel his heart expand again and again. Ngozi felt tense. It was a different kind of tension from the one that had dissolved moments ago. And, like that one, this one had also arisen out of the sudden.

"I feel as if something ... big ... is going to happen," Tony said, sipping now at his bitter lemon.

Ngozi made a small sound and said:

"I've been feeling it for the past few minutes already."

They smiled. It was not a strange thing to them. They felt things together.

Ngozi reached under the surface of the table to a place Tony could not see. A moment later the groovy swing of soulfully softened and intensified hip-hop music rolled forth from speakers that were invisible to him.

The music wasn't loud, nor was it too fast. But it was strong, insistent, sweetly seductive and deeply deeply possessive.

While Tony watched her, Ngozi got up and began to dance. She danced with sweet abandon. She flowed to the music. She did whatever she liked. She was uninhibited. She was wearing a dark-blue Boubou, petered with little streaks of black everywhere which yet did not lessen in any way the dominance of the blue. The dress was spacious and reached to her ankles, and, dancing in it, Ngozi was beautiful. She was magnetic. Inviting.

She stood by the red painting, dancing with rhythmic harmony under the intense gaze of the mountain-lady of the red ocean. Her dance enchanted Tony and more than enchanted him.

He stood up from his chair and sat on the edge of the desk, so as to see her properly. In all that time they'd been together, three years hence, she had never exhibited any such pronounced, uninhibited inclination towards dancing.

This was a new thing. The music was taking over her, deeper and deeper it penetrated. More and more,

more, more. She was swaying, swaying, gyrating. She smiled into his eyes and said:

"I've changed, haven't I?"

He smiled back and replied:

"No, not at all."

She seemed unbalanced and confused by his reply, looked at him steadily for a fraction of a second and then said, with an obvious sigh of relief:

"I'm glad you think so. I'm so very glad. I couldn't bear –"

The door opened and Tanko stood in the doorway, surprised by the person he had been meaning to surprise. His eyes revealed an abrupt shock.

Then hurt. Uncomprehending hurt, comprehending too well.

One look at Ngozi's face told Tony who was standing at the door. Behind were the faces of the six workers in the outer office, all peering through the opened door into the room from which american music was oozing out.

Ngozi felt a shot of embarrassment as, upon the backdrop of the gaping, smirking, shocked faces in the daylight-washed outer office, she felt her eyes imprisoned by Tanko's bemused stare.

Tony, by the force of will-power, remained half-sitted on the edge of the desk.

Like in a film, they remained frozen in their triangle.

By nature Tanko was a possessive fellow. And the music ... and the abandon he had found just now in Ngozi's face, eyes, dance ... and the thin dark man sitting coolly on the desk with a gathered look in his eyes ... – all these struck open an immediate wound in his heart.

He took his penetrating eyes off Ngozi and locked in on Tony. One of them, in the presence of this woman, was an outsider.

Which one?

Tanko, like a predator, canny and cunning, sizing up the strange new male, pounce-ready.

Tony, far from being prey, yet not quite predator, saw in Tanko a hard man; intelligent, with quiet emotions perhaps, but hard. And Tony simply watched, and stayed cool. And sought for a way to subtly outman this man.

A part of Ngozi felt a queer thrill of excitement; another, uncertainty; a third, fear.

All is fair in love and war, my dear.

Then Ngozi smiled at Tanko. Her innocent, heart-touching smile. Only, it didn't look quite so innocent in this moment, and more than touching hearts, it hurt them now. It wasn't a genuine smile, and the three of them knew it.

The moment had turned on them and made each a victim of their own expectations. And desires. And ignorance.

There was a circle here. A circle of ignorance. A circle of impending disaster, disaster of the heart.

Then the co-ordinator in Tanko came to life. He masked the jealous pain in his eyes promptly with the breezy, self-assured smile of the seasoned controller, the cool operator, the smooth boss, and took measured, relaxed steps towards the red painting and Ngozi, its painter, an approach subtly lined with the aura of appropriation, clarification, the claiming of a right. Subtle.

His arms were now opened, slightly outstretched. Come to me, baby. You are mine.

Let him see that you are mine.

Tony saw Ngozi tremble a trifle, unsure, unhappy with what the moment was doing to her. Unresolved. He knew Ngozi too well. He saw her battle with Tanko's powerful demand and subtle threat. Everything, unspoken, was subtle.

And so powerful.

Ngozi tried to break the sudden bond, but was too weak to master the moment. So the moment mastered her. And she yielded to the demand facing her and, under the poetic recording eyes of her Tony, joined with Tanko in a lovers' embrace.

Tony turned his face to the still open door.

The way in is the way out. –

This is when strange things happen, always. The *Igbos* have a saying: *mberede ka-eji ama dike.*

The unexpected shows who the warrior is.

Some say there is in everyone a warrior. Some say there is a war in everyone. The difference is the story of man.

And something strong came alive in Tony all of a sudden. He was the odd man out. Why lie? Life is in the moment and the moment is now. Forever is now. Why evade a deep perception of the actuality of the thing? Why chase the same old chimera all over again?

He had been down this path before. He knew the terrain well. He knew Ngozi too well, and himself even better.

Something something strong came alive in Tony.

The way in is the way out.

Ngozi eyes were chained on him, in them a look he couldn't read. At the door he returned the look one last time, this time with a smile, and walked away.

His victory was a smile, a poet's smile, full of philosophy beyond joy and pain. He left her trapped in the golden loving cage of Tanko's possessive victorious embrace, and walked away.

Chapter 7

...

Somebody wrote:

God created the World in six Days, and on the Seventh He rested. But *who?*

*

Ada and Tony, the twins, sat together in the little dinning table, quietly eating supper. They were not talking. The television set was on. Christmas was being celebrated on all fronts. Every channel was talking or singing or advertising Christmas. Every once in a while, a knock-out, a Banger firework, like a gun-shot, exploded somewhere outside. Usually they banged in threes, fours, fives, simultaneously lit and flung by an equal number of young boys and girls, and sometimes even a mischievous adult or two played along. And a constant festive noise streamed in through the open windows.

The twins were very quiet. It had been a momentous day.

Later, Ada said goodbye and retired to her bedroom. Tony watched TV some more, then went to his own bedroom too.

Thoughtfully, each slept the cool night quietly through.

Chapter 8

...

Nigeria is not an easy country to define. Contradictions abound. Gaps and questions. A collective striving for the unifying theme. A collective striving for decentrification. Each man for himself.

Ngozi reflected on the nature of this country she was about to leave for a length of time unknown to her. My Nigeria. She would miss Nigeria. She was glad to be going. She would visit soon. She would never visit, never return. It was all over.

A people without a past. A past without a people. A people with a loaded history. An indigenous nation with no one indigenous root. A bunch of de-rooted wild flowers, thrown irascibly into one vase, an english vase. Live together or perish as one, in my vase.

There were many things Ngozi had not told Tony. So many things. One was that Tanko actually lived in Germany and only visited Nigeria once in a while for brief periods. Business First, the business centre in Anthony Village, was only one of the numerous money-making ventures which he stubbornly kept operative, inspite of sporadic attacks of losses, non-profits, unbalanced sheets and other hazards that were the fruit of long-distance management. She was going to Germany to *live* with *him*.

Another was that all he, Tony, had to do was simply to claim her, and she'd never leave him. *Just claim me, Harmattan, say something, do something, let me know that you want me and me alone now and forever, and I'm all yours. Together we'll make it.*

But she couldn't tell him that. With them, things happened always only suddenly, unbidden, or not at all.

Or not at all.

Why was she even sitting here with Tanko? She wondered. Under a thatch roof, in a crowded Lekki Beach. Holiday makers everywhere, outdone in their noise only by the music that came too from every-where, mixed into the crashing, washing roaring of the December waves. Tanko was talking. She wasn't listening.

Two days had passed since Tony had walked out on their lovers' embrace. And in another two days' time, she would be in a plane headed for Germany. Tomorrow was all she had, the landing field of pre-cious dreams.

Tanko finally fell silent. He was extremely hurt. He knew that she was thinking of Tony, of whom she had only once, early in their relationship, told him. And ever since the day before yesterday, when he'd walked in on them, she hadn't been the same.

But Tanko kept quiet.

He wanted her too much. And what he had seen in Ngozi's and Tony's eyes two days ago frightened him. Most of her things were already in his flat in Düsseldorf and, in two days' time, she too would. And that was all that mattered.

He wanted her too much.

But in the car on the way home, she said to him:

"Tanko, I'll be out throughout tomorrow."

The evening sun sank softly, beautifully red, behind them.

Tanko cast a short look at the wild, unkempt palmtrees flying past them in mute, waving stolidity.

"Where will you be?"

"Where I must be. Wait for me."

Two things.

*

There were many other things that were said in the car during the course of that drive, but the above words were the gist of it, and the conversation (let us not call it an argument) ended on the note on which it had originally started, which, if it was not clear, was confusing; if not divisive, then uniting; it was either deception or it was simplicity, like so many other worlds.

And so she called on Tony and Ada the next day.

Ada was there but Tony wasn't. Ngozi waited once

again for him. She had to know something.

*

Thursday, the thirty-first of December, 1998, was a day Ngozi would never forget. It was really a beautiful day. The weather was fine, if hot. The harmattan dryness of the air was moistened, softened, by a surprisingly heavy dew fall that commenced in the hours preceding the break of dawn and only let off when the sun had climbed up in the sky, nature gently assuaging in part an involved thirst.

Ada and Tony's house in Festac Town was cosy, beautiful and neat. It was a duplex on 5th Avenue, markedly standing out with its sturdy black gate, decorated by african etchings, and a freshly painted white wall.

Ada first looked long at Ngozi before letting her in.

"How did you find out our house?" Ada asked.

Ngozi smiled, twirled the strong fingers with which the painter in her worked, and said in a voice filled with sweet revenge:

"Ngozi magic."

Ada laughed a little. But today wasn't like the day before yesterday. Something had happened in their new friendship. Something that only women comprehend, without words.

There were no Christmas decorations inside the house. Somehow Ngozi found that oddly relaxing. Thirty minutes, a light meal and a drink later, there was nothing else to do but talk, seal a powerful friendship and prepare to say goodbye for a long time to come.

"When I saw you in that bus, I thought you were on your way home. How surprised I was then to find out that you live in *Festac*."

"I was going to see someone in Ota," replied Ada.

"*Ota!* And don't tell me you still returned to Festac that same day, by public transport!"

Ada shrugged. She was sitting crossed-legged on the carpeted floor, her back propped up against the front of an arm-chair. She seemed most withdrawn.

Ngozi was sitting also with her legs crossed, but upon a sofa diagonally across from Ada. Her short, beaded braids came down her head like a lama's haircut. Both women were extremely relaxed. Not even Ada's withdrawn air tampered with this settled softening within and around them.

Each asked the other about her past, her family, her life. They knew they would soon be parted, and for a long time perhaps. But somehow they also liked each other so much. Just like that. It was like a friendship that had been ever hoping to someday, somewhere, somehow happen.

And now it had. To them. Come too late. Gone too soon.

As they spoke, smiled, sorrowed, traded, they began to see their differences and similarities.

Ngozi, half-pretty, oddly and irresistibly attractive, pitch-black, with a quiet, introspective but powerful aura, was like water in a hot dark cave. And everybody gets thirsty ever and again.

Ada, tall, dark brown, beautifully and sharply featured, impetuous and irritable, intelligent, was like stone. A rare and beautiful precious stone. A cornerstone.

Each contained the other, water, stone, and stone, water.

Ada was laughing.

"Ngozi, tell me the truth," she said. "When you yapped that Area Boy, Dele, in your office like that…, weren't you somewhere in your heart trying to impress me?"

Ngozi chewed back an amused smile and solemnly shook her head.

"What rubbish!" she said.

Ada pointed a discerning finger at her friend and laughed even louder, saying:

"But those his slaps took you by surprise, didn't they?"

Ngozi here sighed.

"My sister, which star didn't I see? And I saw them all twice each, if you remember. Infact, I must paint them one day for all the world too to see. They were special stars, close upon the borders of the untrodden."

Ada laughed, then said, cocking her head:

"*Paint* them? Can you paint?"

"Ah-ah. Hmmm. See you. I even read Fine Arts in school – although I'm not sure if that was fortunate or unfortunate."

"Oho. So you'll soon be speaking like Tony soon."

"No, really," Ngozi continued. "You see, education as we know it is an imposition from without upon the inside. But in this inside, the lives –"

Ada had put up her hand. "Please ... spare me. I've heard it all from Tony."

Ngozi appraised Ada awhile, then shrugged and kept quiet.

Ada wasn't sure if there was any hurting in that silence. And she went on:

"But it's very interesting. I wish I could see some of your works."

"You've seen one already."

It arose instantly before Ada's gaze. She stood up and looked down at Ngozi with serious, contemplative, charged eyes.

"*You* did the Red Painting?"

Ngozi evaded Ada's eyes. The look in them was too intense.

"Why didn't you tell me?"

Ngozi shrugged.

"It's the painting that matters, not the painter."

"I hear!" retorted Ada gently. "That's one of the

most absurd pieces of nonsense I've ever heard. If there were no painter, there would be no painting. The painter is very important."

"Yes, no, that's not what I meant…"

There was a new respect and wonder in Ada's eyes as she studied Ngozi.

"Have you ever done an exhibition?"

"Yes … a few times …"

"And?"

Ngozi shrugged. For a moment another face appeared from inside her face, the face of a stranger, sure of itself but lost in its surroundings. Then it retreated again.

"What is it exactly that you're going to do in Germany, Ngozi?"

"To live. To work. To school. To experience a new life. I don't know. The opportunity came. Tanko played his part. Now I'm off."

"I don't get it …" Ada said, almost to herself. "Naija has opportunities. Why don't you stay? I can help you organise more exhibitions. It's what I do, I'm an event organiser …"

An empty looked crossed Ngozi's eyes. Some iner thought seemed to distract her.

"Maybe one day, in the future, when I get back …"

This was all very vague to Ada. She couldn't form a coherent picture. But then, she reflected, some things are always vague. And, perhaps, it was right so. She decided to leave the matter be.

They kept talking, rivulets of phrases travelling in different directions at different speeds, often interspersed by longer or shorter periods of silence. Most things remained unsaid. The most important things. Like, *Ngozi, you know, Ada, you know, I think I've found a friend in you.*

Things like that are felt, intuitively perceived, but rarely said.

It was time for Tony to get back home.

His sister and the woman he loved decided to prepare a special meal for him.

As Ngozi helped Ada and Ada helped Ngozi in preparing pounded boiled plantain and sweet vegetable soup, with no meat but lots of fish, his absolute favourite dish, Ngozi kept seeing over and over in her mind, the heart-shattering smile with which Tony had left her office two days earlier, whilst she was in Tanko's arms.

And now she understood what had driven her here today. She loved Anthony Harmattan Chikezie.

And no one else. Loved him so much that there could be no middle. Not any longer.

Ada, however, was quietly watching Ngozi. She observed different emotions arrive and depart her features and knew she must be suffering. And wondered what other sufferings yet lay soon ahead of her. For she doubted that Tony had told her the whole truth.

Ada asked Ngozi all of a sudden:

"Do you love Tanko very much?"

Ngozi had already nodded before she could check herself.

"But... *what?*" continued Ada.

"I don't know – Tony is somewhere inside me where I can't reach. Somewhere that I don't know. Like the wind that comes and goes. But I also love Tanko." Ngozi stopped with a surprised look on her face, as though utterly astounded at the fact that just moments after encountering within herself the understanding that she loved Tony and Tony alone, she should find herself confessing truthfully that she loved Tanko too.

Tanko was very different from Tony. Big. Always definite and definitive. Industrious. Clever. Canny. Manfully possessive. A dependable man. A big baby. He was also in her heart.

How strange.

For some time the two women were again silent, lovingly preparing Tony's meal.

This time it was Ngozi that broke the silence.

"Ada, do you have a boyfriend?"

Ada stopped what she was doing for a while, pondered meticulously the question left and right, in and out, then replied tentatively:

"I used to."

Ngozi looked for a way to unlock that reply, then

simply asked:

"What happened?"

"I don't know. I think I scared him off."

Ngozi started laughing.

"Men are such cowards!"

"Such *softies!*"

"Hia!!" they both cried out together, at home together in their circle of laughter.

*

Tony was strolling the streets of Festac. It was that special week between Christmas and New Year. Absorbed in himself, somewhere at the back of his mind he could still hear the smell of the decorated scenes around him.

Unseeingly, long after the time in which he'd told Ada to expect him back, he moved through roads, closes, avenues, weaving this way and that, occupied by his thoughts, his constant companions.

He wondered why on earth people say that no man is an island. On the contrary, thought he, each man is an island, alone, different, unique.

His mind went to Folarin, his unique friend in Port Harcourt. It was many years ago that they had been mates, best of friends, in secondary school. Then, they had been able to discuss everything from the heart. Then, friendship had been magical. But now, people were growing older and growing apart. Tony sighed and longed again for that friendship, that closeness, that healing and uniting brotherhood he had once shared with his best friend, before adulthood clamped down guardedly on everybody's world.

Five minutes ago I was not the person I am five minutes later. And no one knows what happened in those five minutes of separation. Or were they perhaps not ten? ... No one knows for sure.

Tony kept walking. He had now retreated completely into himself.

Everywhere he went there was, covert or overt, what appeared to be joyous festivity. But only fleetingly did it register upon his consciousness. One moment he was moving past the Texaco petrol station on Road 22, the next he was walking past the Church on Road 21, three distinct intersecting roads away. He did not notice the vanishing of large pockets of time, the traversing of intersecting and divergent lengths and bodies of space. He had stopped hearing the generators competing loudly with the music, or smelling the fumes and the roasted chicken weaving drunkenly in the air. He did not see the people, the piled up rubbish here and there, the boys and girls strolling in arranged pairs, the familiar faces of a few acquaintants, nay, nor even the approach of the evening twilight. He didn't see the twinkling lights, the decorations, the Christmas holiday.

Indeed, if there was any other thing of which he took cognisance, apart from his lonely thoughts, it was the sweet, tasty coolness, intoxicatingly dry and dreamy, of the harmattan evening ...

He loved harmattan. The dry season. The dusty, dusky, hazy season that lifted him out of the mundane world of his fellow human beings and into a country, a realm, of buried dreams and risen hopes and the vague expectation of something beyond even the poet's words, waiting for a new world upon which to dawn...

Tony breathed the harmattan, in, out and in, and, if only in this, was happy.

*

Tanko Ibrahim sat alone in his house and sipped at a long glass of very cold beer.

His was a beautiful house, tastefully decorated with the subtle northern touch that was prenatally his. On a fine, cosy rug in the centre of his sitting room he reclined on his side, half-propped up on an elbow, watching and enjoying on cable television a t.v. drama about hearts, faces and love.

He saw himself as being very different from many northerners, perhaps because he had been born and bred in the west. However hard he tried, he could not but see himself as a Nigerian first, a northerner later. And, somehow, he was very happy about this. He treasured this condition of his heart and mind and guarded it jealously. To be anything else, he felt, would be to be less, to degenerate. He truly had come to, with the mature perception of an adult, appreciate and love Nigeria. And hate Nigeria. And love Nigeria. And fear Nigeria. And fear for Nigeria. And love Nigeria. And the mixture was incomprehensible to even him.

And he loved Ngozi because she was special. She was deep, sensitive, a precious flower, and he would guard and protect her always.

But she was also like the wind. She had her own subtle agenda all of the time, and always actualised it. Always got there. So he had to let her be. She would come back. She was his.

Everything he wanted was his.

He was a Nigerian. And every real Nigerian knows that all things are obtainable. This was the magic and the curse of Nigeria. She made a patient, canny, opportunistic optimist of everybody, and the devil take the hindmost.

And he, Tanko, was not a backbencher. He was always ahead of the rest. Winning was a part of him. The early bird sharing the clean riverwater with only its own reflection.

Yet he was also a little afraid.

She was unpredictable. Perhaps because she was an artist. Perhaps because she was an easterner. Perhaps simply because that was just how she was ...

Brother, a wind.

*

Tony braced the beautifully cool evening breeze

with a half-smile upon his features as he gradually turned his thoughts towards turning his footsteps home. His footsteps home.

It was good this way, felt he, good that he wouldn't see Ngozi again before she left upon the night of the morrow.

It was best like this.

*

The deliciously, lovingly prepared meal was cold.

Ada said to Ngozi:

"I wonder where Tony is."

"I hope he didn't go to my office," replied Ngozi.

"No," said Ada, "he didn't go there. But I don't know where he went."

"He always keeps me waiting."

They lapsed into silence.

It was a silence that yearned for something, something born often out of silence.

They knew what it was. It became clear to them and, while they waited for Tony, they sought him out and went to him, in his poetry.

Contact was what it was.

Let us hold hands and form a circle, Tony, all three of us. Until you find your way back home.

Ada retrieved from Tony's bedside the six sheaves of paper that he had given her on Christmas Eve, and which she had returned the day after. And for the first time, she realised with alarm that she really had no poems, no other works at all, of his. She must remedy that .

She put the papers in Ngozi's hand, who noted that there was a seventh, and it was titled On this we stand. They smiled. The seventh would be the first.

More than victory was this smile. It was Understanding.

And then they sat down together, side by side, and entered again into his heart, soul-sisters, heads locked together over cherished words, in a world of their own, like it was in the beginning...

On This We Stand

Did you love me, did you not?
My, what a heart...
Did it break, broke it not?
I do not know –

Is it ending, is it beginning?
Hard to tell...
'Tis forever my love
Forever we are this –

This? What is this?
It is this:
Please be true to your heart forever.

This wasn't actually what they had expected

And when they had read the poem, Ngozi wished that she had read it alone. She and Ada looked into each other's eyes and Ada would have said sorry if she had been able to form the word.

The poem was Ngozi's. Alone.

*

Tanko had dozed off.

The half-empty glass of beer tipped over and spilled on his face, jerking him back awake. As he came to, he inhaled some off the beer through his nostrils and was seized by a choking, wheezing, coughing, gasping spell.

When it was over, he calmed down, turned over and dozed off again.

He dreamt of Ngozi. She had two faces. At first she had only one, looking at him, smiling the familiar smile. He smiled back and turned away. But as he turned back to say something full of love to her, he thought he caught sight of another, totally different face there... but it was quickly replaced by the original one he knew, smiling the familiar smile.

He smiled back again and turned away fully.

Then he slowly, unobtrusively bent his head around and stole a look back again at her – he saw...

Tanko screamed and awoke again. He was breathing somewhat heavily.

Then he stood up and walked to the television set. It was still on but he did not see it. On the tv was a framed photograph. He lifted it up and gazed thought-fully at the familiar face of Ngozi, smiling her special tender smile. Exuding an inner radiance more beauti-ful than a dream.

*

Finally Tony got home, lighter of heart.

He let himself in through the gate. There was a little garden of sweet-smelling lemon grass, carpet grass and a thrush of orange torch lilies. By them was an acorn tree stubbornly at home and at peace with itself in this little space, as though the house had met it there and not the opposite. Its upper roots bulged, like rising shoulders, out of the earth and, sooner or later, if it wasn't brought down, it would bring the fence down, beside which it had, two decades ago, suddenly began to grow. They had inherited this house when their parents died some years earlier. It was all they had and, for now, all they needed.

Tony liked his little garden and it seemed to him that he always drew strength from it and, strangely, gave strength to it too.

Now he stood looking at the few orange torch blossoms amidst their fluffy, slim leaves, and inhal-ing deeply the rich aroma of the lemon grass. The fact that he watered the garden twice a day, coupled with the intermittent rains, gave harmattan a hard time of settling down here. It was a battle here between man and nature, harmattan against Harmattan, Tony struggling against himself. The war within.

But it would get cold, very cold at night, and the dust-laden harmattan from far north in the Sahara would embrace and silence everything. The garden might not dry up, but the harmattan season would have its way. There would be no new blooming, there would be but the sleep.

After a few seconds of standing in the darker shadow cast by the acorn tree amidst the crispy brown and red leaves it had shed between morning, when he had last watered and raked, and now, Tony turned to walk up to the front door. One more brown leaf, in the rustle released by an abrupt gust of cold wind, floated down from the half-clad branches of the mighty tree and came to rest a few steps to his right. His eyes rested on it for a moment, then he approached the front door and let himself in, with the purpose of getting the rake and the waterhose.

He saw Ngozi first and stopped short. By now it was quite dark outside, behind him a blue-black modernity-dotted wall against which he stood silhouetted. The brightness of the fluorescent lit sitting room gave the fact of her unexpected presence a powerful aspect of inevitable, inescapable reality, otherwise called perhaps fate.

By her side on the sofa he saw his poems.

He shut the door and entered.

Ada appeared at the kitchen door and glowered at

him.

"Is this your *two* o'clock?"

Tony glanced at a wall-clock. 8p.m. He blinked, surprised. True, the sun had set on him and it was now dark outside, but he just hadn't thought of the time.

Ngozi was looking at him. He walked to her, took her hand and pulled her up.

Ada turned around, walked back into the kitchen.

"I've been waiting all day for you," Ngozi said.

"I've been thinking of you all day long."

The curtain lifted. Suddenly again it was the moment.

They were standing close to each other. Like two days before, she wore a boubou, this one milky grey and calm. She looked up at him from under her beaded braids and waited for him to kiss her. She had been waiting for the past three days. For the past four years.

He lifted a hand and, with his thumb, caressed once the corner of her two lips, where they met up stage right; exit or entrance? Did she tremble just a little?

Her heart sank as his hand dropped, his voice asking:

"Ngozi, do you love Tanko?"

She took a little step backward and nodded.

"Do you love me?" he asked her next.

She inclined her head to one side and wondered why he loved taking long, torturous routes in life.

Seconds sped on ahead of other seconds.

She didn't answer his question.

Somehow, he didn't expect her to. She had never once answered him that one question. Even in the old days. If only she would. It would make everything easier, childlike as that sounded.

Ada appeared at the kitchen door again. Ngozi exchanged a look with her, disengaged, smiled at Tony and said:

"Guess what we made for you."

"What?"

"Guess!"

"Pounded plantain with vegetable soup?"

Everybody laughed and eyes met quietly.

*

At 8:40 p.m., Ngozi and Tony set out on a stroll.

They walked in silence for a while.

As they stepped into Road 51, Tony said:

"When you are gone, I'll become able to concentrate again on enjoying the harmattan."

As though she didn't hear what he said, which she knew was a contradiction, if she knew him well, she said:

"How come there was so much tension between the three of us in the house just now, while we were having dinner?"

He looked at her.

"Was there?"

The evening was light upon them and cool around

them and gentle within them. It wasn't the world alone that was slipping away, but they too experienced between them a feeling of sundown, an eveningtude, the ending of a little era.

"What haven't you told me, Tony? Is there someone else?"

Anthony felt a touch of irritation. How come women could sometimes read him so easily.

"Maybe."

She stopped and peered searchingly, through his eyes, into his heart.

"You know you're mine," she said to him matter-of-factly.

"No," he said, "I didn't know that. Infact, it's news to me."

"You're mine, Tony. Who is she?"

But then again, women were like instruments. This was Tony's belief. Once you understood the instrument and mastered the technique and subtle art of playing it, it would always bring out just the melody you want, everytime.

"I don't know. It's a complicated story."

They were strolling again. The night itself, independent of the human beings decorating it, had come alive. This then lent a sharpness to all the sights and sounds around them. The music coming from drinking spots and barber shops, the lights of salons, the head- and tail-lights of the cars passing by, the sound of each engine and the throbbing of the presence of humanity; Festac people, strolling the streets of Festac, talking Festac gist, passing the evening away.

"Do you love her?"

Tony heaved a deep, heartfilled sigh and answered truthfully in a low voice:

"I love her beyond words."

Like a black arrow, poison-filled, so did jealousy pierce lightning-quick the opened heart of Ngozi. She inhaled sharply and said:

"Oh."

He was watching her closely. He saw her every expression, read her every reaction. He shared her pain, like he shared everything else with her, including his heart. He patiently waited to see how this evening would end. There was too much love in his heart. He couldn't afford to err again. Not again.

They turned into Road 22, keeping to the Post Office side of the road.

They held hands. For different reasons, they held on to one another, unto the moment. Curiosity and fear, and love the unifier.

"Where have you been all these years? What have you been doing since you aborted school? You went to Ota, to stay with your cousins... then you disappeared. No communication again from or about you. Tell me. What was?"

What was? Hm. He liked that. Brief and all-encompassing, this simple two-word bi-syllabic question. What was?

Poetry was.

"Nothing and everything," he replied softly.

They walked on in silence, on and on. Ngozi did not say anything. They turned right into Road 32 and then turned left again into Road 41, parallel to Road 22, and began going in the opposite direction to the one in which they had been going. It was a much quieter road than 22, although they ran parallel to one another.

Like she knew he eventually would, Tony went on: "Have you ever been to Ota?"

"No."

"Half-village, half-city. My cousins live in the G.R.A. there. The streets are untarred. Beautifully at peace with nature. It must be the most neglected G.R.A. in the country. I have a friend there who says that there is no other G.R.A. in Nigeria that fits the popular acronym 'Government Rejected Area'. If it's a Government Reserved Area, says she, like it is supposed to be, the Government must have had very strong reservations about it from the start!"

She looked at him, wondering why he was doing this. Says *she*. He had a faraway look in his eyes and a small smile on his face, and she wondered if he could really be unconscious of what he'd just nonchalantly done. He had just told her that he was missing someone in Ota. Why was he being so cruel?

"But I like the place," he said. "I love it. It's very quiet there, and yet the City-centre, hm, if I may call it that, and even Lagos itself, are not that far away. One a bike-ride, the other a bus-ride, away."

"What do you mean by even Lagos itself? Is Ota not in Lagos?"

"No, it isn't. But quite a number of people don't know that, because it's so close. It's actually in Ogun State, just beyond the boundary. I worked in a little school there, teaching english and music. Otherwise I wrote poetry. Ngozi. I wrote and wrote until I there was nothing more to write. That's when I returned to Lagos."

"When was this?"

"Last month."

"Oh. Just last month?"

He nodded.

"I would like to see the poems you wrote there."

"Would you?"

She gave him a funny look and said nothing.

"They aren't here," he finally said. "They are all in Ota."

"I thought you never went anywhere without your books." She looked at him pointedly. She didn't believe him. He wanted to hide something.

He looked at her. His gaze was open and earnest.

"This time I didn't."

She believed him. She had simply doubted at first because she knew how little he often interested was in showing his work. Or maybe because she knew that there was another woman in those poems. Who was she?

"Do you intend to live now in Lagos again, then?"

"Uuh, I'm not decided yet. Folarin wants me to come down to Port Harcourt, even if only for a while. I don't know."

"Folarin!" her eyes lit up. "How is he?"

"Doing fine. I spoke to him, was it two or three days ago. He told me to say hi. I told him our paths had crossed again, for a second time."

They continued in silence all the way down to the junction of Road 41 and 4th Avenue. There was something about the last sentence that drove them to reflection.

"You remember that riddle Folarin used to ask people back in those days?"

"Which one?" laughed Tony. "All his words were riddles."

"When are two halves equal to three halves?"

Tony's laugh changed to a smile.

"Oh, you remember *that!*"

"I remember many things, Tony."

He nodded slightly and said, "But that was a special one. A different one. Do you remember what that was all about?

"Something about destiny," she said lightly, her eyes watching him.

"Yeah, " he said, his voice becoming amused. "We were searching for the mathematical expression of our theory that destiny always makes the same thing happen three times in order for its two halves – the seeking and the finding – to be resolved."

She smiled and shook her head.

"There you go again. I remember the crazy things you guys used to say. Halves and two-thirds and units. Three halves make a whole. Twice is never enough. And all that. The derailed pseudo mathematicians."

"Ha! That insult is a contradiction of itself."

"So was your theory."

"That twice is never enough? Really?"

Their eyes met.

Point raised, she changed the topic.

"I read some of your poems some days ago, in the bus. When I met Ada. She was on her way to Ota, right?"

"Yeah," he said. "Normally, nothing would induce her to go to Oshodi. But it's simply the simplest and shortest route. Mile 2 bus-stop to Oshodi, Oshodi to Sango-Ota."

"And I just read them again now. It is still you, but freer in structure. Freer."

"I'll give you more tonight. I wrote them yesterday and today, and the day before. Take them with you.

Let them connect you to me, me to you."

As he said the words, he clutched her hand even more tightly. They turned, stopped and looked into each other's eyes.

Still she saw the hesitation in his eyes. Why? It was all locked up in the time in Ota, the years he'd spent there, she felt. If only he would go deeper in telling that story. But he didn't want to. That much was clear. To her.

Now she started speaking.

"You know, after we parted... I started reading Sylvia Plath."

They had moved on again. But instead of going forward, Tony had turned them around and they were going back.

Now he turned his head sharply and stared penetratingly into her. He remembered her depressions, knew only too well the depth and intensity of her emotions, the conflicting nature of her varied perceptions. This was why he was so unsure, why he kept delaying the very thing he was hoping for. She was a very good actress. So good, in fact, that even she herself was deceived and taken along. She could mask her indecisiveness and hide her ignorance. So well, that one in the end did not know if she was as clear as she seemed to be, or if she was just telling herself lies.

This was the problem. He didn't know. And she wouldn't say. She left it to him to do the deciphering, but he knew that he couldn't, couldn't trust his own judgement in this. Once bitten, twice shy.

Now he asked:

"Why?"

"Everything."

"I learnt from Hemmingway the value of life."

She knew what he was talking about. They had really experienced one another deeply in those days in the university. The highs and the lows. Besides, there was also the vow.

"I hope you've learned the same from Plath…" he continued.

After a moment of silence, she said;

"For a while I laboured under the urge, it filled me. It consumed me. I toyed daily with the idea. Then I realised that I was approaching the whole thing from the wrong side. The sought thing was life, wasn't it? Release, freedom, life. That was also what finally reached me in and out of her works. The intense struggle to break even. Spiritually. Then I knew what to do. I had to take up the struggle too in my own life. It is the world's struggle, and it is the individual's struggle. To find the Light! And, through her, I had got a glimpse of the ways to take and the ways to avoid, and received the determination to try! And each day of my life on earth is a victory, however much sorrow it brings. Everytime I go through and emerge with the longing unquenched and the certainty, somewhere at the back of my mind, that it is the earth which will, in the right time, sever itself from me, and not I flee from it, then I am winning. Then I have won! Am I getting through?"

Tony smiled.

Anyone who didn't know what they were talking about wouldn't know what they were talking about. Deeper than life after death. Life before death. Life over death. Life and only life. Life, forever.

"Can artists be separated from their works, do you think?"

"The question is," he replied, "Can artists be united with their works?"

"I would have liked to have known her."

"*I would not* have liked to have known Hemmingway; definitely."

She laughed.

"Either way," said she, "we are here now again. The prophecy was not fulfilled."

"Wasn't it?"

"Are we dead?"

"Are they still alive, those two people from the university?"

"Anyway, we made the prophecy ourselves."

"Let it be, Ngozi. Life won. What else could we hope for?"

She reflected that this wasn't a bad way for it to end.

"How's your health?"

"I'm really alright, really. Done all the tests."

"Okay. But you're still so thin. You have to eat a lot and often. Eat everything you can lay your hands on."

"*Everything?*" he cocked his head at her.

"If you can lay your hands on it, and it's healthy and looks good, yes."

He looked into her eyes and saw Pandora's box pulsating. She saw thirst in his eyes, so intense that she suddenly felt her river begin to flow down, quivering. She looked at him and all her thoughts were begging him to take her, and finding in it hard to believe that he could not hear them, these shouting thoughts.

They looked at each other. He still hadn't got used to this new side of her. The person who just spoke was the person who, two days earlier, had danced. Who was she? What happened to the shy soul that had once been there? When and how did it get out of the locked box?

Tony did nothing. And they walked on. At that moment, Nogozi did not know whether she loved or hated him.

In both their hearts they perceived the continuing fatality of their odd love. They both knew they were hiding many things away from one another. Yet they had just said the most important things. Often encrypted, yet spoken. Dissolved. But the very manner in which they were doing it, itself contradicted the resolving. In a way it was as though they both knew that they would surely part and part tonight, that they were too strongly tied up in different directions. And yet they longed to snatch something from one another, from the moment, this moment, something they would both treasure forever, whatever forever was, however long people say it lasts. And there was also the hope, distant but real, that perhaps if they *touched* just this once, it would sever each automatically from all other engagements. Yet there was also the fear that if they ventured too far, they would spoil everything, even the past and the memory of the past.

And what more beautiful thing can you have beside the past? The memorable past to which we look back full of nostalgia. If you spoil your past, then all you have left is only the present, the elusive present, the fleeting moment, the hardest adversary of all. The realer it is, the finer. The finer, the more elusive, more uncertain. The principle universal. The more uncertain, the less we know and know for sure. We waste the moment trying to figure out the moment, never plunging in, never ever. So make your past memorable. Live with your heart today. Never push your heart aside. Tomorrow, your heart it is that will remember, and mourn, and ah, I wish...

So they hovered in this middle, two philosophers, loving each other heart-painfully but not knowing what to do with this love. Should they leave it clean, 'undefiled' – would it be better so, better to remain 'just' friends ? Or should they consummate it, and take a step in that other direction?

Or should they wait again?

And what of Tanko? And what of the unknown woman of whom Tony remained most reluctant to speak?

So they each waited for the other to make the last move first. To break completely the barrier. And waiting, they waited, and waited in vain.

Goodbye.

Chapter 9

...

They parted the following evening at Murtala Mohammed International Airport. It was New Year's Day. A stiff affair it was. On one side stood Ada and Tony. Facing them were Ngozi, very withdrawn, and Tanko.

Tanko and Ada looked into each other's eyes again. The shock of recognition had left an impression in each. The dark eyes and the big eyes. But the more they looked, the less they saw as they both quickly retreated ... until there was no curiosity any more, only knowledge. Thoughtfully they looked away from each other, preferring not to touch eyes again.

Ada brought her hand out of her handbag and handed a slim book to Ngozi. She looked at the title. *Nocturnes*, by Leopold Senghor.

She raised her eyebrows at Ada.

"You might need that sometime," Ngozi said with a shrugged smile. Ada laughed and handed it over to Tanko.

"I think you'll need this more, my dear," she said to him with a smile. He looked at the cover and his face lit up.

"Hey, this is great stuff!" There was surprise in his voice as he looked at Ada. And it occurred to her that he was a very different person than what she had thought just a moment ago, and she thought also that he glowed when he smiled. She glanced at Tony, and saw that he had looked away.

At a point Tanko went to make some final check-in. When Ada was not looking, Tony and Ngozi exchanged a look that was full of pain and silence, and then he gave her a little note-book. She slipped it into her hand-luggage.

Not long after, Tony and Ada left.

*

In the bus on the way back home, Ada asked:

"What happened between both of you in the university?"

"We loved each other too much."

"What does that mean?"

"We both swore that we could not live without each other. And that we would always be there for one another and each would always protect the other even unto death. And that we would rather commit suicide than live apart – as you can perhaps observe, we meant it."

He turned his face her way and saw the expected look of disbelieving horror on her face.

"Pretty gory, isn't it?" he asked.

"More than that."

"On the contrary, actually. The opposite is what is gory. When people who love each other are not able to believe this, to love so passionately, to make this vow. With or without words. Because then, what's the point?"

She was silent a while. The bus was dark and over-crowded. And it stank.

"And what finally happened?"

"That's what I'm waiting to find out."

The bus, a small Volkswagen, swerved to avoid a pothole and hit another. The bump was hard and merciless and threw the passengers first head-first towards the ceiling of the bus and then buttocks-next back unto the hard wooden benches.

Curses thundered at the driver and his conductor. They and their families were cursed and savagely abused, and if words could kill, no member of his family would have seen the light of day upon the morrow. And words can kill. This is the tragedy. No wonder the world is full of dead people. We have all murdered ourselves and one another with our words.

Haven't we?

That's what I'm waiting to find out.

"I think I know," said Ada.

"Know what?"

"What happened next."

"What?"

"The harmattan gave way to the rains."

"And what does that mean?"

"That's what I'm waiting to find out."

*

When the plane was in the air, Ngozi got up from her seat and headed for the ladies' room. Hours had passed. She gathered that they were over the Atlas mountains now.

The toilet was well-lit. She put the cover down, locked the door and sat down. On the cover of the notebook she saw the words: *Tony Harmattan – Dance Again.*

She began to read. She went from one to the other without once reading any twice. *Dance again... Young... The touch... Earthly moments... Seeing through... Young again...*

Because she had already read the last two before, under memorable conditions, they were doubly special now. She remembered the bus-ride. Had it been just a few days ago that it had taken place? It seemed, so near in the poems, so far in time.

Then she read the next poem: *On this we stand.*

On this we stand...

That poem. Contact. Much too close.

Now she read it alone, without Ada's presence disarming her, her eyes questioning her. And she loved it. *Please be true to your heart forever.*

I will, Tony, I will.

*

Tanko wondered why Ngozi was taking so long in the toilet. He got up and walked over. Surreptitiously he knocked, lightly, on the light panel of the door. He wasn't sure, but he thought he heard the sound of rustling pages.

He made to knock again but something seemed to hold him back. He walked back to his seat. Sitting down, he placed his right palm on the window-seat next to him, her place.

Soon after, Ngozi returned and occupied again her former seat. In her hand was a strange blue notebook. He looked at her quizzically.

"Were you *writing?*"

"No," she answered.

They looked at each other for a while.

He raised an eyebrow. She said:

"Just going over some thoughts."

"Whose thoughts?"

"Mine."

Again the raised eyebrow.

"I didn't know you kept a diary."

"We all do, Tanko."

She wasn't looking at him, but past him.

Tanko kept silent and inclined back into his seat.

Ngozi turned to the window, reopened the book and turned the pages slowly to where she had stopped, interrupted by the knock she had known was Tanko's.

She was confused. The coolness of the cabin air

seeped into her body and softened her thoughts. The soft soft hum of the aircraft seemed to separate her soul from her body. She was all alone.

She reached above her, turned on and directed her light, like she had done her thoughts and her heart, on Tony's poems, shielded away from Tanko, everything shielded away from him, and read his whose thoughts were always with her.

Circles of Experiencing

Oh dear,
She's back, again
Is she?
How deep
Within?
Sea
All these deep things in our hearts,
Oh dear
What is love?

One surprising day
It will find its end
Its start
Walk again
Circle of one love…

Did she ever go?
I'm there again –

Ngozi turned her head and saw Tanko watching her.
    She turned back and read on:

Never Stop

When stop
Breaking their hearts?
We didn't mean to do it.
But it hurts,
Hurts
When we break another heart

Vow
The last
Shall be the last
Break no more
Not like this
The type we can avoid
A little self-control

Sad
I wish I hadn't broken her apart
Yet hearts will continue to break
To heal
We will continue to grow

The last shall be
The last yet sadly

The first

Meet again, smile again, yearn again
Ever and again
Splinter heart into a billion stars
Tomorrow it will shine again
Heart, love again

Never let them stop you from yearning
Light, life, that laughter
You laugh
O love, my dear, did I ever tell you
That I love the way you laugh?

I love the way you laugh.

Ngozi smiled all the way from her heart, and read on.

It was the same smile Tanko had seen in his dream the day before, the smile that was proceeded by an alien look. That dream was still on his mind as he watched the inky blackness outside the window. He had for a while tried to sleep, but to no avail. Now he brought out the book Ada had given them and tried to read, but his mind would not settle down. His thoughts were still on the smile and the look that had been her face in his dream.

And if he had looked up a moment earlier, he would have seen that face again. Now he saw neither the smile nor the look, but observed only, when he looked up, too late, her head bent over the strange blue book.

Our Dance

She dances like water, as though she were drunk,
At home on the floor, in a world of her own,
Flowing and still, melodious, sweet funk,
Reflecting my joys all the way to the bone

And when she so dances, she dances my dance
I watch and I'm dancing along in my mind
Forever is here in your movements, your stance
But there in your eyes I see that you are blind

We see you so clearly but you see us not
We love you so dearly, but this you feel not
You dance on, alone; yet, strange: we mind not,
For we love you most in this way – do stop not

But I see much deeper, ah, I see your heart
I enter it gladly because I love you
And in there I dance all alone, all apart
Forever I dance on and on within you

The heart is often a very baffling thing, and most baffling of all is the heart of woman. How does she know? How can she be sure? How did she arrive at her answer? *What* does she want?

Ngozi's mind was already made up as she quickly turned her eyes to the last poem, dated 1.1.99, the day of her departure.

The end of the road.

The Conquest

From mountain to mountain, valley to valley
Island to island, what seek we?
Who are we?

Like pain it rolls
It rolls like pain
Like pain it rolls within my heart

The more I swim, the less I hurt
The more I laugh, I win.

Ngozi was clear. Very clear. An ice-cold anger that blazed through her heart and burned a path for her thoughts through her mind. A wintry calm.

She tore one page after the other from the notebook, each rip, each severance a violent scar upon the soft economy night-quiet. A few heads turned. But she went on with what she was doing until she was done.

Tanko watched her closely. Watched the cold, angry, yet calm and relaxed look in her eyes. A contradiction of sorts: she seemed resolved, unencumbered, happy, determined. *Defiantly?*

She dumped, stuffed, the ripped pieces in the back of the seat ahead of her. Tony's poems would inhabit the skyscapes forever and a day, however long that was, they would fly … but not with her.

"Is everything okay?"

It was as though scales had fallen from the deep eyes through which Ngozi returned Tanko's gaze. Her thoughts spoke to her. One was a poet. And one was a man. And she knew which one she wanted. There was poetry everywhere, moving poems all over, but real men were few.

For the first time since the sun rose over twenty four hours earlier, she felt that she was truly in a new year. Suddenly yesterday was conquered. She held Tanko's hands and nodded, her eyes never leaving his. *Everything is fine.*

He nodded at the back of the chair in front of her and said:

"What was all that?"

She pulled up the arm-rest between them and yielded totally to him and his quiet strength and replied calmly:

"Just old thoughts. Yesterday's dreams…"

*

Harmattan lay awake all night, monitoring the flight of the bird. Monitoring its heartbeat. And, gratefully, disconnecting. It was all over. He was free. He could start again.

There was no electricity, so he lit a candle. Then he put pen to paper, and wrote:

Whisperings

Whisperings of a new return of harmattan...
Is it hazy? Was it foggy? Dark, bright?
Feels, like Dawn, Sounds, like Dawn
Looks, like new Dawn –

An early breath of Harmattan serenaded
My heart –
Birds accompany, airy prose
Crickets nonstop chirping
Yet night is gone ~
Deeply I love the boundary between
Rains and thirsty Harmattan...

Nature has said yes,
Why say no?

The aeroplane touched down in Frankfurt early in the morning. Outside it was snowing and the darkness was lit up by the airport lights.

Ngozi awoke with a jerk and a wild jump of the heart. A solitary renegade of a heartbeat inside of her. She said something. But when she was fully awake, moments later, she could not remember what it was she said. But Tanko never forgot it. – Aye, now he really *knew.* The ache would stay in his heart for the rest of his life, deeper than knife, as ephemeral as dream, with no context in which he could ever share it with her, with anybody.

And his victory too was a smile, an introspective smile.

She snuggled up to him. Slowly he put his arms around her, firmly, and his eyes looked out of the window, the deep gaze in them full of unanswered questions about life.

*

Ada lay on her bed at dawn and thought carefully about her brother and about her new friend and about the big man with the curious, familiar eyes and about all three of them and about all four of them.

She decided not to tell Tony what she knew. The time may last long, but one day it would manifest, and maybe, then, everybody would be mature enough to deal with the story. In the end, it was but an everyday story. But all this she would have to keep to herself and watch him, even while he suffered.

So, did she understand or was she taken by surprise when he said to her, after breakfast:

"Ada, I'm going back to Ota."

Ota. G.R.A., Ota. The home of the poet in him. he was going home to himself. And to the other half of the poet in him: Ronke, the quiet woman, the village waif, the school teacher, the one that calmed his heart, the one of whom he never spoke.

The windows were open, through it, clearly visible, the chalky whiteness that had become the world and the sky. A fine, thick haze smothered visibility, the air was dusty, sharp and sweet, and very cold.

There was a look in his eyes. Detached, hungry, lonely, resolved. *Defiant?*

She turned her eyes and gazed into this harmattan-bedecked morning-view of the world. It seemed as though everything was submerged in chalky-white haze. But if you brought your gaze lower, away from the light grey sky with its barely discernible tint of blue, down towards the earth, you saw the electric cables and telephone wires and the houses in the nearest vicinity, all wearing an aura of dreamy isolation.

Each seeming to be alone. Each seeming to want to be alone. Apart from every other. But was or was it not an illusion? The harmattan, like everything that comes from the desert, is a master of illusions.

All that lay farther away than the houses and wires was invisible in the sweet white of harmattan. But, once one saw the nearby things, one was comforted, did not feel completely deserted, understood that when the rays of the sun, rain-makers, finally broke the power of the haze, everything, near and far, would appear again, as they were before.

Nothing would change, yet nothing would be the

same again for having slept in the arms of the harmattan winds and awakened again, renewed, repossessed of the power to actualise the dreams laid or fortified in our hearts by the distant songs of the sojourning harmattan, the stranger from the north.

Ada knew why he was going to Ota, just like she knew why Ngozi was going to Germany. He was not going to see Ronke. She was not going to be with Tanko. Tony was going to commune with the season he loved most, in the place he loved most, with himself, in peace.

And Ngozi was going to come again.

And Tanko?

Words fade. Forms crumble. Substance remains. Harmattan and rain. The sun rises higher in the January dawn. It is the sun. Did it set yesterday? It rises as though a new story were on the arising, and not the old one that it still is. The sun is shinning on the same old houses, the haze disperses on yesterday's dreams and the clouds gather in the south.

Everybody thinks their own thoughts, but who knows what?

The undefined what.

Che Chidi Chukwumerije

The Poems

Whisperings (prologue)   6
Dance again   13
Young   14
The touch   16
Earthly moments   18
Seeing through   24
Young again   27
On this we stand (chapter 3)   41
Circles of experiencing (chapter 4)   60
On this we stand (chapter 8)   105
Circles of experiencing (chapter 9)   128
Never stop   129
Our dance   131
The conquest   132
Whisperings (chapter 9)   134

The End

...

Twice Is Not Enough

...